THE RUNAWAY STORM

DANIELLE STEWART

Copyright © 2015 by Danielle Stewart

All rights reserved.

No part of this book may be reproduced in any form or by any electronic or mechanical means, including information storage and retrieval systems, without written permission from the author, except for the use of brief quotations in a book review.

THE RUNAWAY STORM

For five years Jamie has managed to outrun his past, his pain, and anything remotely resembling an emotion. Now, with his probation over, he's finally ready to leave town with plans to fade into the crowd and noise of Las Vegas. No more court-ordered grief counseling. No guardian trying to keep him out of trouble. He's convinced all he needs is a blackjack table and a strong drink for the rest of his life.

Trixie believes she can tame the monster that keeps her tethered to Las Vegas. Her boyfriend, Eli, is difficult, but she can handle him. One night, however, her child's in danger rather than herself, and she realizes running is the only chance they have to survive.

Jamie offers safe passage out of town on one condition—Trixie cannot pry into his past. With every mile they drive, they grow closer. But the storm that chases them won't relent, and somehow they must find a way to weather it together.

PROLOGUE

For the last five years Jamie felt like a dog tied to a tree. Through the hot summers and the freezing winters he'd been tethered out in the elements. He'd tugged against that rope for so long, and now finally he was free. Racing down the highway, weaving his way through the traffic, he felt as though nothing could stop him. The radio blared. The wind cooled his face. For the first time in a long time he had no one to answer to. No one was begging him to open and bare his soul in the name of healing.

His phone rang again and he knew it was Travis. He'd put the poor guy through hell since he moved into his house as a teenager. It was still a mystery why he'd ever bothered to defend him. Jamie smoked, stole, ran away, and pretty much did anything he could to convince Travis he was a lost cause. But it never worked. The harder he pushed Travis away, the tighter he held on.

Maybe that should make Jamie want to stick around with Travis for the long haul. Shouldn't there be some loyalty to the foster dad who'd kept him alive? But what Jamie was doing—finally leaving—was the gift he was giving to Travis. The thank you he could never really bring himself to say. Travis had found something special when he met Autumn. He deserved happiness, and Jamie wouldn't stand in the way of that anymore.

Being pissed at the world was contagious, and he didn't want to pass his plague on to the new happy couple. His probation was finally over. He was free, and he could run. He'd already run from his past. He'd run from anything that resembled an emotion, and now he was physically running the hell away. It was time to be a faceless and friendless zombie, lost in the masses. One destination seemed perfect: Las Vegas.

CHAPTER ONE

Jamie tapped his finger against the cloth of the blackjack table, indicating he wanted another card. This wasn't a game of chitchat, but not everyone could understand that. They'd socialize with the player next to them, act like they give a crap about the dealer's real life, or worst of all think they had a shot with the cocktail waitresses.

Blackjack was a game of numbers, nothing else. Jamie had figured that out when he was fifteen years old and spent the last six years perfecting his game. It took a good amount of self-control not to laugh at the players who sat down next to him with lucky charms or gut feelings. This game had odds, and if you paid attention you could swing them to your favor. So far, over the last two months, he'd done just that.

"It's my night," a loud-mouthed southern man chanted as he slapped the table and shimmied his body down onto a stool. Jamie knew he couldn't actually keep someone from joining a blackjack table, but he let his dirty look give it a try. The man ignored him as he laid his money on the table and waited for his chips.

Mickey, the dealer Jamie had come to like for his ability to shut up and deal, didn't acknowledge the man. He continued with the hand he and Jamie were in the middle of and flipped the cards with lightning-fast skill.

"Hellooo," the jackass cowboy hollered again, banging his hand on his money.

"You're coming in the middle of a hand sir; you'll need to wait just a moment," Mickey explained, never looking away from the chips and the cards that were in play. Jamie split the two aces he'd been dealt and blocked out the ignorance wafting over to him from the other side of the table.

Mickey slipped a couple cards out of the shoe. Two face cards, two black jacks to be exact, and a large payout for Jamie. The stack of chips piled up in front of him, and Jamie did the math quickly in his head. He'd turned a thousand dollars into ten thousand in the last two days.

"Now can I get some damn chips?" the hick asked with a roll of his glossed over eyes. His hair was swept over to the side to try to cover up the balding spots, but it wasn't working. His sweat-covered scalp was still glistening under the sparkling lights of the casino. "This looks like a hot table. I think it's a good time to get in."

"Good for you maybe," Jamie grunted as he bit at his bottom lip to keep more of his angry words from spilling out.

"What's that's supposed to mean?" the man asked, narrowing his eyes at Jamie as he collected his chips.

"Everyone reads the blackjack books but no one gets to the chapter about courtesy to another player. I've hit a rhythm here, and you're about to disrupt it. The right thing to do would be to wait until this shoe is over then jump in when he shuffles."

"Oh, is that so, junior?" the man scoffed. "I've been playing this game longer than you've been alive. I don't need any pointers from you."

"Clearly." Jamie sighed. "Cash me out, will you Mickey?" He sat back and let the dealer collect his chips.

"Oh, I scared you away did I?" the man asked, chewing on his toothpick like a hungry horse. "Or is it past your bedtime, kid?"

Jamie knew there was absolutely no room for emotion in gambling, including anger. He'd been sitting at these tables for the last two months, and this guy would be catching a plane out of Vegas in a few days probably. It wasn't worth getting tossed out of this place just to school this piece of crap.

"Hey. Hey you," the man called out, shifting his attention away from Jamie, who was ignoring him, and toward Trixie, the cocktail waitress. He reached his arm out and grabbed her shirt. It sent the balanced tray on her hand wobbling, but like a pro, she steadied it. "Sweetheart, sit down with me. I'll drink all those drinks, and you can be my good luck charm."

"I'll be back by in a minute to grab your order." Trixie smiled, tactfully wiggling out of his grip.

"I don't want you to bring me a drink; I want you to sit with me," the man pouted, reaching out for her again but catching only air.

"You going to do anything about this, Mickey?" Jamie asked, cocking an eyebrow at the short curly haired dealer.

"Nope," he replied flatly. "We've got security for that. My job's just flipping cards over and handing out chips."

Jamie shook his head and looked down at the chips that had just been handed back to him. Ten one thousand dollar chips. "I guess I'll cash one of these in for a few more hands then."

"Changed your mind, junior? That's good. I didn't want to lose your good luck." The cards began to fall and the chips quickly got plucked away one by one from the man who went from cocky to tight-lipped.

When Trixie came back with an empty tray, Jamie knew she was walking into a trap. The man had fallen short on his bets, so he'd need to compensate with some macho bullshit.

"Baby doll," he said, looping one arm around Trixie's waist, "I need a good luck charm. Sit down."

"I've got a lot of drinks to serve. What can I get you to drink?" she asked, not even wincing under his tight grip.

"I'm a high roller here, sweetheart. Your boss would want you sitting down here. It's part of the package. I paid for you."

She laughed as she touched one of his shoulders flirtatiously. "Trust me, cowboy, you couldn't afford me. Now tell me what you're drinking so I can take care of you."

"Take care of me. Now we're talking. Just hop on my lap here." He pulled her onto his legs.

"Let her go," Jamie said, pushing his stool back but hesitating before he stood.

"Mind your business, kiddo. This is grownup shit happening here. I've spent plenty of money tonight. I deserve a little company."

"She's not a prostitute. She's a cocktail waitress," Jamie bit back.

"Jamie don't," Trixie said sternly, waving him off. "Don't bother." Her eyes implored him to back off, but he couldn't.

"So you two are on a first name basis?" the man asked, grinning like he'd just stumbled upon some pertinent information he could use in his favor. "You should have told me there was a line to take a run at her. I'd have waited."

"Actually I'm not stupid enough to convince myself just because a girl smiles at me she wants me. It's her job to be nice to you, but not to sit on your nasty lap. So let her go so she can do her job." Jamie stood and from the corner of his eye he saw Mickey gesture for the pit boss.

"Don't worry, buddy boy, you'll get her back when I'm done with her. She might not want some kid once she's had a real man, but that'll be your problem." He reached up and touched Trixie's rouged cheek, and she broke character, recoiling at this touch.

"Is there a problem here?" the bald-headed broad-shouldered pit boss asked, looking first at Jamie then at Trixie.

"No," Trixie cut in quickly. "I was just on my way to get these gentlemen some drinks. Good luck, cowboy." She smiled, shimmied off his lap, and grabbed her tray.

"Trixie," Jamie said as she hurried by him. She ignored his words. Her cropped blond hair bounced as she moved quickly away.

A few minutes later she was dropping a rum and coke in front of him. "Don't get in my business like that Jamie." She huffed. "I need this job, and if the pit bosses think I'm pissing off high rollers I'll be out on my ass. Just mind your business."

"Trouble in paradise." The man chuckled and tapped the table for another card, breaking every rule by hitting on seventeen.

"Cash me out, Mickey," Jamie said.

"You sure this time?" Mickey asked with a tiny smile that grated on Jamie. This place was like nowhere else on earth, and some nights that was welcomed, other nights it bugged the hell out of him.

"Yeah, I'm sure. No reason to stick around here. I'm up, the table turned to shit, and the waitress has an attitude. Better call it a night."

He took his chips and left the table, hearing Trixie walking quickly behind him to keep up. "Wait a second Jamie," she pleaded, but he barely spared her a glance. It wasn't until she was tugging on his sleeve that he finally stopped.

"I heard you loud and clear, Trix. Sorry I thought maybe you didn't want to get groped tonight. I'll mind my own business next time."

"I appreciate you trying," she said quietly. "It's pointless, and it puts my job in jeopardy, but I still appreciate you speaking up. It's nice to have a familiar face here every night. I don't want to see you get tossed out for fighting."

Jamie couldn't help but get sucked into the rare violet-blue of her eyes. It was probably just whatever fancy makeup stuff she'd put on that made them pop in such a powerful way, but it worked. He couldn't help but stare into them any chance he got.

"Why do you even work here?" Jamie asked. He knew his questions were blunt, but that was how his brain was wired. It made sense to him. If you want to know something, ask it in the most direct way possible. "Don't you have a husband or a boyfriend or something?"

"I do." Over the last couple of months he had noticed she seemed to have grown accustomed to his candor, at least enough to answer rather than just walking away like some people did. This time she softened her face and let her silky skin crinkle around her smile. "You don't beat around the bush do you?"

"Why would I? Life's too short. I'm wondering why, if you've got a guy or whatever, you work here instead of him making enough money so you don't have to get groped all night."

"First, I don't get groped all night. There are plenty of boring, uneventful nights around here. Second, Eli is out of work right now. He's in construction, and he hurt his back. This job works for me; I can be home with my little girl during the day." She fiddled with her tray, giving her explanation awkwardly.

"Sounds like a story I've heard from a hundred girls." Jamie flipped his baseball cap around and tucked his money into his pockets.

"Just call me a statistic, I guess." Trixie sighed. "I'm going on break now. Do you want to go outside for a smoke?"

"You smoke?" Jamie asked, looking her over.

"No, but I know you do, and I'm sick of being in here. I just need some air. God only knows why I'd want to sit out there with you, since you only seem to be capable of insults."

"I'm not trying to insult you," Jamie said apologetically as they moved across the loud casino floor toward the exit. "I say what I think. Everyone assumes I'm an asshole, but I'm pretty much just being honest."

"My mother used to say people who claim to be brutally honest are far more brutal than honest. Does that sum you up?"

"No," Jamie said, grabbing his pack of smokes from his pocket. "It's not up to me to make people feel good. I tried that for a long time, and it never helped anyone. Now I just say the first thing that comes to my mind."

She nodded as though his explanation was enough to forgive his bluntness. "I get that. I'm always trying to make other people feel better, trying not to make waves. I'm jealous that you're able to speak your mind."

"So are you?" Jamie said, flipping his lighter up and taking a long drag from his cigarette. The end burned as bright as the lights of the towering hotels around them. People bustled by, all heading in and out of the casinos like zombies. It was the middle of the night, but you'd never know it here.

Before Trixie could explain, Jamie fell forward into her, a thud to his back sending him flying. He grabbed her two silky soft arms and steadied her the best he could. "What the hell?" he barked as he spun around and saw the drunken jerk who'd just slammed into him.

"Exactly," the man slurred out. His greasy matted-down hair looked like it had been pressed flat by hours in bed. Foam gathered at the corners of his narrow lips, and he tried to work out what he should say next.

"Eli," Trixie shrieked, her voice getting eaten up by the endless noises of the Vegas strip. "What the hell are you doing here? Where is Maisie?"

Jamie watched Trixie's eyes fill with frantic tears. She shoved Jamie out of her way and went nose to nose with Eli. "Where the hell is she?"

"Shut up," Eli grumbled, shoving her back, her body thudding into Jamie. "She's in the truck. Why do you have to be so dramatic all the time?"

"You drove like this?" Trixie cried, gesturing to his

hunched shoulder and inability to keep himself from swaying like a boat in a storm. "You put my daughter in the truck and got behind the wheel like this?"

"I'm fine," he spat back. "Let's talk about what you did." He slammed a fat finger into her chest. "Who the hell is this?" He gestured over to Jamie. "You're supposed to be working, dropping drinks at tables, not screwing around with losers. I'm stuck at home, babysitting your little brat while you mess around behind my back? That's why I came here. I knew it." He lunged forward and grabbed the strap of Trixie's snug tank top. She clamped her hands down on his wrist, but she was no match for his tight grip as he pulled her into him. "You're coming home. We're leaving right now."

"No," she yelled, digging her heels in and swinging one arm back to try to grab anything that could help her. She got a handful of Jamie's shirt, and he locked his arm with hers as tight as he could.

"Let her go," Jamie demanded, but Eli wasn't listening. His oxen stature dragged them both across the sidewalk and farther away from the casino. People stopped and gawked like they were watching street performers rather than domestic violence. Jamie's mind spun, trying to form a plan. This guy had at least fifty pounds on him and the advantage of being drunk enough to not even feel whatever punch Jamie threw.

Luckily though, help had arrived. Two brick-wall-sized men in black polos, wired devices in their ears, charged toward Eli. They didn't say a word. No warning was given. With quick precision they peeled Eli's hands off Trixie and placed their bodies between the two of them.

"Sit on the curb," one of the men yelled, pointing at the ground as though he'd only be giving that instruction once.

Eli moved toward Trixie and, with a swift swipe of his leg, one of the men took him to the ground.

"I've got to get to my daughter," Trixie blurted frantically and stared out at the enormous strip, loaded with thousands of people, trying to deduce where he would have parked the truck containing her daughter. "Where is she?" Trixie dropped to her knees so she could be at his level. "Give me the keys and tell me where you parked. It's hot Eli. She can't be in the car. It's too hot."

Trixie was right. Even though it was the middle of the night the temperature in Vegas this time of year never dropped to anything comfortable. A little girl in a car could suffocate.

"Tell me what's going on, Trix," one of the security men said as he pulled her to her feet. "You guys have been warned about making a scene here."

"Lou, he drove here drunk with Maisie in the truck. He left her out there somewhere. I need to know where he parked." She ran her hands through her honey-colored hair as though she might pull it all out any minute.

"Son of a bitch," Lou said, shaking his head angrily. "I'll have to call the police, Trix, you know that. I've covered for you enough times. If your daughter is in danger, I've got to let the cops know. You're going to lose your job over this, and you know he's going to get off without any trouble."

"Why?" Jamie asked, finally chiming in.

"Just get him to tell where she is. Do whatever," Trixie demanded. Tears were pouring down her cheeks, mixed with thick black mascara. "Jamie . . ." She turned around and stared at him, desperate for some kind of help.

"It'll be all right," he assured her. "What kind of truck do you have? I can check the closest parking garages."

"It's a piece of shit truck, more rust than red paint, and missing the front bumper. I'm guessing he'd have parked it in the top level of the East Plaza garage, but I don't know for sure." She spun around as the security guys were yanking Eli back up to a sitting position. "Is that where you parked? The East Plaza?"

"I don't know," he slurred. "Yeah, that's where it is, but I don't know what level."

Trixie jammed her hand in his pocket and fished the keys out, ignoring whatever gross statement he made about her action.

"Trixie, you should stay here and wait for the police," Lou instructed as he put zip ties on Eli's hands behind his back.

"I'm going to find her," Trixie announced and broke into a full sprint toward the street. Jamie had to aggressively brush by a herd of tourists in order to not lose her.

"Wait up," he shouted, banging his way past more people. When she reached the parking garage the crowd had thinned out, and he was able to meet her stride. "You take the elevator up and start looking for the truck there. I'll start at the bottom, and we'll work our way toward each other. We'll find her twice as fast that way," Jamie explained, trying to get a very distracted and frantic Trixie to listen.

"Yeah," she nodded her head hysterically, "that makes sense. But who takes the keys?" she asked, looking at the shiny objects in her hand.

"You take them; if I find her and it looks like I can't wait for you or the cops, I'll smash the window. Just go," he said, having to nudge her into the elevator. When the doors closed and he knew Trixie was on her way up, he started racing through the garage. Sweat was beading across his forehead, and he could only imagine what a little girl in a hot truck must be feeling like. He ran as fast as his legs would carry him up and down every aisle. Then when he cleared the first floor he yanked open the heavy metal door and took the stairs to the next level, skipping two steps at a time.

Three floors later he spotted it. The truck was parked sideways, taking up three spots; one wheel was up on the small cement block meant to stop people from pulling in too far. He raced toward the truck and skid to a stop at the passenger door, accidently slamming his body into it. There, slumped over, was a tiny-framed girl in a crumpled up white nightgown, her brassy hair matted down with sweat. He strained his eyes to see if her chest was rising and falling, but he couldn't tell. Starting with a light tap on the window, he finally let his fists begin to bang, trying to get her attention.

"Mommy." He heard her gurgle out the name as her head fell backward and her eyes slit open.

"Unlock the door," Jamie said loudly. "It's too hot in there. You need to unlock the door."

"You're a stranger," Maisie gasped, her eyes going wide and her little hands coming up to her mouth.

"No, I'm a friend of your mom's. Her name is Trixie, and your name is Maisie, right?" He tried to talk calm enough to not scare her but loud enough so she could hear him clearly through the glass.

Her tiny shoulders relaxed slightly, but she made no move for the lock on the door. Jamie could see the wheels in her head spinning, cycling through what she'd been told to do over and over again when dealing with a stranger.

"It's too hot in there, Maisie. Can you feel that? If you don't want to unlock the door at least roll the windows down a little. Your mom is coming. You just have to trust me, okay?" Jamie put his palm on the glass and moved his face closer for her to see, as if there might be something in his eyes she could believe.

"Jamie!" He heard Trixie call out, her voice echoing and bouncing off the large cement pillars of the parking garage.

"Over here," he shouted, tossing both his hands up so she could see him. "Your mom's here, Maisie; open the door." He watched her little fingers yank the lock, but she couldn't pull it up. "The keys, Trix, give me the keys."

As Trixie rounded the front of the truck she tossed the keys to Jamie, who immediately slid them into the lock and pulled the door open. Maisie practically collapsed into her mother's arms, and they both slid to the ground, leaning against the truck for support.

"She needs cold water. You need to get her inside," Jamie urged, but he knew his voice wasn't penetrating the cloud of relief that surrounded Trixie now. "Come on," Jamie crouched and touched her arm gently, "she needs to cool down."

"I have to go," Trixie said suddenly, as though she were waking from a dream and realizing she'd overslept. "Give me the keys. I've got to get out of here, right now."

"Slow down," Jamie said, closing his hand around the keys before she could grab them. "Security is going to call the cops. Let Eli get arrested for child endangerment and assault for the way he was dragging you around. The only thing you need to worry about right now is getting Maisie cooled off."

"No," she said, pulling herself to her feet. "You don't understand the situation. Eli's father is a U.S. Senator. He will do anything to keep Eli from becoming a scandal before the next election. You have no idea the lengths he's already gone to in order to keep Eli's mistakes from hitting the papers. When the cops show up, he'll make one phone call, and it will be me getting arrested. He'll take Maisie, and I can't let that happen. I need to get out of here. Just give me the keys."

"You're going to leave in his truck? And where are you going to go?" Jamie held the keys so tight he could feel the sharp metal digging into his hands.

"I don't know. I can't go back to the house. He'll be able to get someone there before I get through the front door. I'll have to figure it out." Trixie lifted her daughter and shifted her onto her hip.

"Do you have money?" Jamie asked, knowing Trixie was not thinking this through at all.

"Eli has all my money. He doesn't let me have access to it. I've been putting away some tips, but he found them last week. That's why he was spooked. He thought I was cheating on him. He has control of everything. I have nothing."

"Then you can't just leave." Jamie knew he was sounding matter of fact, but there was a growing need to be realistic.

"He could have killed her," she whispered. "I've always been able to take his crap when it was just me. I knew what I could handle, and I've always found a way to make it through. But she is my whole world, and I'm not going to let him hurt her again."

"He has a right to her though, doesn't he? You'd be breaking the law by taking her from her dad, right?" Jamie thought through each pitfall to this gut reaction.

"She's not his," Trixie explained. "He has no rights to her, and he's never wanted any. It's me he thinks he owns, and his father has done everything in his power to keep Eli's evilness quiet. Now give me the keys so I can get out of here."

"You're going to leave in his truck with no money and no clothes. Do you really think you're going to get far? He'll have you arrested for carjacking. Leave the keys here," Jamie said, slamming them down on the hood of the truck. "Come with me. I'll drive you out of here, as far as you both want to go."

Trixie's mouth opened and then closed again, like a fish out of water. "You can't do that," she said simply. "I don't really know you."

"And neither does he. No matter who he has in his corner, he's not going to know to look for my car or my credit card. I know you think I'm an ass . . ." Jamie paused when Trixie looked up and waved him off.

"I don't think that."

"Then get in my car, and let's get out of here. I've won a shit-load of money at the tables in the last couple months. My car has a full tank of gas. If you want out, I'm your best shot." He extended his hand and waited, worried she might not take it.

She didn't. Instead she handed her fragile and exhausted daughter over to his open arms. "I'll grab her booster seat."

Jamie pulled a small pocketknife out of his pocket and flipped the blade open. Crouching down, balancing Maisie in his arms, he punctured the firm black rubber of the front tire.

"A little head start won't hurt."

CHAPTER TWO

"Lou," Trixie said breathlessly into her phone, "I need you to keep Eli there a little while. Do a shift change, take a break or something. I need a little time."

"Trixie, you know the second he gets next to a phone he'll be calling Daddy, and this thing is not going to go well for you. It won't go well for any of us."

"I know. That's why I'm leaving. I have Maisie, and I'm getting the hell out of here. All I'm asking for is a chance. Please Lou, do whatever you can."

"I'll put him in a holding room for a little while, and let him sweat it out. But you know as well as I do, I'm going to pay for that."

"I'm sorry, Lou."

Trixie hung up the phone and turned to see her daughter staring wide-eyed back at her. "Do you feel okay, honey? Are you still hot?"

She was clutching an ice-cold sippy cup of water and a Popsicle Jamie had grabbed from the gas station. "I'm not hot," she said through her orange-rimmed lips. "Where are we going, Mommy?"

"We're going on an adventure, baby. Doesn't that sound fun?" Trixie smiled so wide Jamie wondered if the little girl could see through her efforts.

"What about Silky Bear?" Maisie asked with a quiver in her voice.

"He can't come," Trixie apologized, swallowing back a lump of sadness. "We don't have time to go back home."

"Because Eli will hurt us?" Maisie asked, her voice sounding far more adult than it had a moment ago. The words cut at Trixie's skin to the point she had to cover her heart with her hands.

"Silky Bear is going on his own vacation," Jamie cut in. "I saw him packing up a little suitcase and his beach towel. He's going to send you postcards though."

"Really?" Maisie asked, and Jamie saw a flash of excitement on her face as he glanced into the rearview mirror.

"Yep, he's taking a bus, and he said everywhere he stops he'll put one in the mail for you. He was really excited about his trip."

"That's good," Maisie said, hugging herself with her tiny arms.

"And he told you to have fun on your trip too. He was a very chatty bear before we left. But you know that." Jamie's casual tone seemed to balance the energy in the car.

"He does talk a lot," Maisie agreed.

"Do you like Pinky Poo Princess?" Jamie asked, flipping open his center console and pulling out his tablet. With his knee on the steering wheel he used his hands to navigate the screens and pull up the show. He yanked a pair of headphones out and plugged them in.

"I've never seen that," Maisie said, craning her neck to try to see what he was doing. When he handed the device back to her waiting hands, her eyes lit with excitement at the beautifully animated pink bubbles and dazzling crowns. Within a few seconds she was engrossed in the show and giggling like only a petite curly headed girl could do, half squeal and half breathless gurgling.

Trixie's face was pressed to the window, her shaking shoulder the only thing Jamie could make out. Her hands were like a nest she buried her face in, and every few seconds a tiny whimper would make its way to his ears. For a man who always had something to say, even when no one wanted to hear it, right now he couldn't come up with anything. He clicked on the radio and brought it to life. A low country song came through the speakers, and he tapped his fingers to the beat against the steering wheel.

Watching signs on the highway whiz by, he didn't bother reading them. He was heading east. That was all he knew. It didn't matter what town they were blowing past; he had no intention of stopping until they needed gas.

"Sleep a while," he said quietly, grabbing his sweatshirt from the back seat and handing it to Trixie. "I've got six hours of that show she can watch. You'll need to drive later so try to get some sleep now."

Trixie used her delicate fingers to wipe away her tears and gather herself. She glanced back one more time at her daughter, who let out another giggle.

"Where are we going, Jamie?" she asked, rolling the sweatshirt into a pillow and resting it on the window.

"It doesn't matter," he replied, still staring straight ahead. "Just sleep."

CHAPTER THREE

After a couple hours of fitful sleep Trixie stirred, shooting upright in a panic. "Maisie," she gasped, and Jamie clutched her shoulder before gesturing to be quiet.

"She's been out cold for about an hour. I turned off the show when I stopped for gas." He watched the panic melt off Trixie's face.

"This is crazy," Trixie said, running her hands over her bluntly cut bobbed hair. "We need to just go back. Eli is going to lose it when he finds out we're gone. I can tell him what he wants to hear, and I can calm him down when he's sober."

"He'll kill you eventually, you understand that, right?" Jamie asked, the direct nature of his words returning. "Or he'll kill her." He gestured back toward Maisie.

"You know how people can tame lions?" Trixie asked, turning her body so she was looking right at him. "You go to the circus, and you see this lion do all these tricks. That's what Eli is. He's an animal, but if I can just remember what to do and how to get him to listen, then he can be around people. We're safe if I do that stuff. But this—just leaving—it'll make him crazy, and he will hunt us."

"And every now and then someone at the circus gets eaten," Jamie retorted, "because you can't really train a wild animal. There is no fixing that. But, if you want to go back right now, I'll take you. It's up to you." Jamie prayed Trixie wouldn't make him turn the car around.

"I don't even know you, Jamie. I have nothing besides the tips in my pocket and the clothes on my back. What are my options? Should I just pull into some small town and go live in a homeless shelter with Maisie?"

"We're driving, Trix," Jamie said, gesturing to the wide-open road in front of them. "We're driving until we can't drive anymore, and we'll get you whatever you need as we go."

"How?"

"I've been winning at that casino for over two months. I literally have a trunkful of money and absolutely nothing to do with it. You can have a completely fresh start."

"How did you win? No one there really wins. I'm there every night. People go up and then get greedy and lose it all. Did you really win?"

"I count cards," Jamie admitted. "I've been able to do it since I was about fifteen. It's not foolproof in a big casino like that, but I'm good enough to turn a little money into a little more. I lose just enough to keep the eye in the sky from noticing me, and I always walk away when I'm up. Greed and luck mean nothing to me. It's science. I came out here to make a bunch of money, which I did. I don't need it all, that's for sure."

"I don't even know you," Trixie repeated, and he could

feel her scrutinizing the profile of his face as he looked straight ahead. "Why would you do this for us?"

"I've got nowhere else to be," Jamie confessed. "I have no family, no job, nothing to keep me in any one place for too long. It doesn't make a difference to me where I am as long as I don't have someone prying into my business all the time. I know chicks want to know everything about everyone all the time, and they try to find all my dark secret pain. I promise to help you and Maisie make a fresh start, as long as you promise not to bug me all the time, trying to figure out *what my deal is*. I have no deal. As far as you're concerned I have no past. I have nothing except what you see right here. Deal?"

"So you're saying I can't ask questions like why you have six hours of Pinky Poo Princess on your tablet. I can't ask why it is you're so good with my daughter?"

"Exactly," Jamie said, lifting his chin a little and clenching his jaw to let her know he was not about to answer with any details.

"Okay," she shrugged, "I can live with that. But I won't just take your money. I'm not a charity case. We'll make some kind of arrangement so I can pay you back or work it off some way."

Jamie looked at her curiously, and she blushed like a cherry lollipop.

"Not that," she said, waving her hands and stuttering. "I mean—I'm not offering, just so we're clear. If that's what you have in mind then you can pull over right now and let us out."

"I don't want to sleep with you," Jamie said flatly. "I don't pay women for sex. I don't need to. If you really want to work off what I'm giving you, then you can open a bank account for me. I've got some stuff I need to do with this money, but I don't want it to lead back to me."

"Is it illegal?" Trixie asked in a whisper as though the police might somehow be able to hear her.

"No," Jamie said, shaking his head. "It's just private. You open the account. I'll put the money in and set up direct payments to the places they need to go. For your trouble I'll help you and Maisie get settled somewhere you can be safe."

"And then you'll leave?" Trixie asked, blinking away worry at the idea of being alone. "Is that your plan?"

"I've been tied to the same place for a while, and I finally don't have to be there anymore. I just want to move around, see things, and make money. That's about the only plan I have right now."

"Why were you tied to one place?" Trixie asked, cocking an eyebrow at him. Her features were so delicate Jamie wondered how her skin stayed so perfectly soft with all the worry she had to carry around all the time.

"You're breaking the rule already." Jamie turned the radio up and let the music create a wall between them. She'd have to talk too loudly now to be heard, and that would surely wake up Maisie. Trixie shrugged her shoulders and flopped back into her seat, staring out the window instead.

"I'm going to need to sleep soon," Jamie said when the song finished. He turned the radio back down. "I saw some signs for a resort up here a little ways. Does Maisie like to swim? I'm sure they have a pool."

"She doesn't know how to swim, and she hasn't had many chances to be in a pool, but I'm sure she'd love it." Trixie looked back at her daughter and smiled for the first time since they got in the car.

"We can run into the store and get her a puddle jumper. That's the best kind of float for her size."

"And I'm not supposed to ask how you know that, right? I'm just trying to make sure I'm clear on the rules," Trixie teased.

Jamie leaned over and turned the radio back up. The sun began to crest over the horizon, and Jamie grabbed his sunglasses. Rolling his aching neck from side to side, he focused on the next twenty miles. He was tired; his adrenaline was finally wearing off.

Trixie would get the hint if she wanted this to work out. His past was not open for discussion, and he wouldn't spend all their time fielding questions. They'd have to live in the moment, and she'd have to deal with it.

He took the exit for the resort, and, as they made their way up the winding driveway that led to the main lobby, Trixie craned her neck to look at the large marble pillars.

"We aren't staying here, are we?" she asked, looking at him as though he was about to tell her it was all a joke.

"Just for a while. Let Maisie play around here today; we'll crash for a while and get back on the road sometime tonight. It's better if she's sleeping for most of the car time, don't you think?"

"Yes," Trixie agreed and kept herself from asking how he might know the best way to travel with a four-year-old girl. "Jamie," she said as he pulled the car up to the valet.

"Don't make me turn the radio back on," he said, rolling his eyes.

"Thank you," she whispered, leaning in and kissing his cheek gently. "My whole life people have been letting me down. I've been letting myself down. I've been letting her down." She looked back at Maisie. "I want a fresh start. I never thought I'd have it, and here you are, giving it to me."

"She isn't disappointed by you," Jamie assured as he rested his hand on her knee. "Moms always worry they're letting their kids down, but if you ask her she'll have nothing but amazing things to say about you. You're her hero."

Trixie wiped a few more tears away and nodded her head as she bit down on her lip. Taking his hand, she looked at him in such an earnest way that Jamie had to turn his eyes away. "Right now you're my hero."

CHAPTER FOUR

"I bought you a new cell phone. I know you turned yours off, but that's not good enough. If Eli is really as connected as you say, and he wants to come after you, that thing will lead him right to you." Jamie tossed a new phone down onto the lounge chair next to Trixie, who was watching Maisie play happily in the shallow end of the pool. She'd been reluctant to get a bathing suit for herself out of the swanky hotel lobby store, but Jamie had insisted. Now he was glad she did.

Her trim and tan body was perfectly toned and the hot pink bikini looked as though it had been designed specifically for her curves.

"Thank you," she said, picking up the phone and tucking it into the bag he'd bought for her. "What should I do with this old one?"

"We're going to go to the front desk and put it in the mail. We'll turn it back on and ship it to Wisconsin or something. Let him chase it down."

"That's smart," Trixie smiled. "I hope that's enough to work."

"It'll be fine," Jamie assured as he pulled off his shirt and sunk into the lounge chair next to her.

"Did you get any sleep?" she asked, handing him a bottle of water.

"I'm good. I got a couple of hours before I went to the store. I bought some stuff and made a reservation for dinner in a few hours. Does Maisie like Italian food?"

"She loves meatballs." Trixie smiled. "She's only been to one or two restaurants though. We didn't eat out much. Eli liked us to be home."

"Why did you stay with him? He's not even her dad." Jamie swigged back some of the cold water and slid his sunglasses from his forehead to his eyes.

"That's a loaded question, but most of yours are." She looked over at him and shook her head. "Maisie's dad, Marco, died in a motorcycle accident a few months after she was born. He was the best man I ever met, and the person I thought I'd spend the rest of my life with. We got married right after high school; my family didn't approve. They thought I was crazy, but they'd always kind of thought that about me. So when I lost Marco I didn't feel like I had anywhere to turn, and I started working at the casino. Eli used to be a frequent visitor to the tables, and I swear he had his life together then. He came from such a good family, and he took Maisie and me in without a second thought. I was just so desperate to have back what I'd lost with Marco that I was only seeing what I wanted to."

"Not very smart," Jamie said flatly.

"How do you not get punched more?" Trixie asked, tipping her sunglasses down her nose so she could get a better look at him.

"Hey, this is me, take it or leave it." He waved down the waitress walking by and ordered a drink. "You want anything?" he asked, but Trixie shook her head no. "Okay, add a strawberry banana virgin daiquiri for the kid."

"No problem sir," the woman said, jotting it down. "Does your daughter want whipped cream and a cherry on it too?"

Trixie cleared her throat to answer, but Jamie didn't skip a beat. "Of course she does," Jamie replied. "What kid doesn't want that?"

"Of course," the waitress winked and disappeared quickly.

"That's probably going to happen a little bit," Trixie said apologetically. "We should figure out what we want to say."

"Why do you think you owe anyone an explanation to anything? What do I care if that stranger thinks Maisie is my kid? Things don't matter as much as you think they do. That's half your problem."

"I'm just glad you're here to let me know what my problems are." Trixie laughed, sounding slightly annoyed. "Should we get a list going so we don't forget all the things I've screwed up or have done wrong?"

"No," Jamie said, adjusting his chair back to a more reclined position. "I have a photographic memory. I won't forget any of them."

She stared at him, waiting to see if his serious face would break into a smile. The only thing he offered was a tiny sideways smirk that she'd have to figure out how to interpret.

"You're something else, Jamie." She waved at Maisie, splashing wildly and singing a song from the Pinky Poo Princess show. "Do we know where we're going yet?" she asked, blowing Maisie a kiss.

"Do you have any family or friends you think would be able to help you out? We could head toward them if you did."

"I don't talk to my parents, and I'm an only child. I've been out of touch with everyone else since I started seeing Eli. No one would be excited to see us. I'm not saying no one would take us in, but anyone I would go to, Eli would know to look there."

"Any place you've always wanted to live?" Jamie asked, signing the receipt the waitress handed him and grabbing his ice cold drink. He placed the frozen kid's drink on the tiny table and pointed at it so Maisie could see it was for her.

Her face came alive with excitement, and she charged over toward them, dripping a little train of pool water behind her. "That's mine?" she asked, clapping her hands together hopefully.

"Sure is," Jamie said, skillfully unclipping her flotation device and wrapping her in a towel. He lifted her up and placed her by her mother's feet on the lounge chair as he handed her the drink.

Trixie's eyes were on him again in that way that was begging to know more about who he was. There was no radio out here to drown her out, so he could only hope she'd heed his warning about prying into his past.

"So," he asked, "where would you live if you could go anywhere?"

"I've never been anywhere but Vegas and where I was born in Scottsdale, Arizona. I have no idea where I'd want to live if not one of those two places."

"That's pretty boring," Jamie said. "But I've never been to many places either. I was stuck in my hometown for a long time."

"Where is that?" Trixie asked and when he tilted his head looking annoyed she threw up her hands. "Oh come on; that's too much information? Seriously?"

"Yes," Jamie insisted. "It doesn't even matter. All that matters right now is where you want to end up."

"I'd like it to be somewhere kind of quiet," Trixie said, looking up at the sky as if it might give her some inspiration. "I've never seen snow before. I'd like to go somewhere to see the leaves change too."

"That's a good start," Jamie agreed. "I know the East Coast pretty well. Maybe New Hampshire? I've been to a few places there. They have mountains and lakes."

"That sounds nice." Trixie breathed out. "I could see living on a mountain. What do they have for jobs though? I know it sounds weird, but I don't have many skills. I had Maisie not long after high school, and I've only really waitressed and did retail and stuff."

"What's your dream job?" Jamie asked, sipping on his drink.

"She sings," Maisie chirped through a mouthful of whipped cream. "Mommy, sing to him."

"No baby," Trixie said, waving off the idea. "I haven't sung in front of anyone for years."

"Let me guess, Eli wasn't a fan of you singing for people?" Jamie rolled his eyes but instantly felt bad when he realized he'd hit the nail on the head.

"Good guess," she nodded. "But that's no way to make money anyway. I'm talking more about something that can support me and little Maisie-pants here. Something that's not as dependent on tips. Feast or famine is a cruddy way to live."

"There'll be time to figure all that out, but at least we have a destination: New Hampshire."

"New Hampshire," Trixie looked a little excited by the idea, "that's where we're going to live," she explained to Maisie.

"It sounds better than *old* Hampshire," Maisie reasoned as she sucked up half of the frozen drink before plucking the cherry off the top and eating it.

"It's way better," Jamie assured her as he stood. "Who wants to go on the lazy river? I think they have tubes big enough for all of us."

"Me!" Maisie shouted, hopping to her feet.

"How about you?" Jamie asked Trixie, putting his hand out to help her up.

"New Hampshire," she said one more time, as though it was a snack she was eating and trying to decide if she liked.

"You'll love it," he assured her as he pulled her up and laced his fingers into hers. There wasn't any gesture of lust or making a move on her. It was a silent motion that told her, *I've got you.*

CHAPTER FIVE

"Where are we?" Trixie asked as she stretched the ache out of her back.

"We just crossed into Nebraska," Jamie said and rubbed his tired eyes. "It's about nine in the morning. I don't think between here and Iowa there will be too many resorts to stay in, so we might want to pull into the next decent place we can find."

"That sounds good," Trixie said, reaching back and putting the blanket that slipped off Maisie back over her legs.

Jamie's cell phone rang, and he instantly hit the silent button on the side. "We need to open that bank account today."

"Sure," Trixie said. "That's the least I can do for all the help you've given me. Is that the bank calling you or something?"

"No," he replied flatly.

"Oh sorry, don't turn the radio up. I won't ask anymore, but I do want to talk."

"About what?" Jamie asked, a bit of annoyance in his voice.

"I don't know. Nothing in particular really. I just feel like talking."

"That's a fundamental difference between men and women. I never feel like talking just to talk. That seems so pointless." Jamie knew his words struck people. That was kind of the point. He wasn't looking to be likeable. The thing with Trixie was that she was fully capable of just ignoring his rudeness and plowing on to the next thing.

"It's a way to connect with someone. It's what life is about, not feeling so alone and so isolated. It's important." She turned in her seat to make her case more effectively.

"So start talking," Jamie said, gesturing like he was giving her the floor. "Just don't get mad if you see me reaching for the radio."

"Well, what's not off limits?" Trixie asked, tossing her hands up like he was so difficult to deal with.

"Anything from the last two months."

"Okay." Trixie sighed, tapping her finger against her chin as though she was giving it a lot of thought. "How did you learn to count cards?"

"I didn't learn in the last two months, so you're stepping into a gray area, but I'll answer because I think if I don't keep talking I'll fall asleep. I have a photographic memory and a high IQ. When I was younger it didn't help me much in school, but I figured out quickly if I used it right I could make some good money. I've been working on my game, waiting for the day I could get to Vegas. I was able to turn two thousand dollars into almost eighty thousand."

"What?" Trixie stammered and then covered her mouth,

realizing she might wake her daughter. "How is that possible without anyone catching onto you? I know the security that works there, and eighty thousand would have sent up a lot of flags. They'd have been watching you, assuming you might be counting or something."

"I spread it out over the course of the two months. I made sure to have a few nights where I lost a decent amount and made it back a couple days later. The problem with most card counters is they forget to lose. They buy in at the end of a shoe or actually pick and choose which hands they want to play. It's greedy, and it tips people off."

"That's impressive. The one thing the casino zombies lack is self-control. They get ahead of themselves, and the second they start to win they think they're a prince or something. I've seen guys come in acting pretty normal, and by the time they have a couple stacks of chips in front of them they're talking to me like I'm their personal servant. It's why I don't gamble. I've seen people lose it all or win and treat people like dirt. No up side to that. Well, besides what you figured out."

"It's about focus too," Jamie continued. "I can't let every pretty waitress who walks by me catch my eye. The casino is good at trying to sway you toward distractions and VIP this or that. I just sit there, do the math, and take the risks according to the statistics."

"How long would you have stayed if it weren't for what happened with me and Maisie? Would you have kept making more and more? Did you have a plan for all this money?" Trixie looked completely dumbfounded by the idea of someone actually outsmarting the thing she'd always imagined as impossible to beat.

"I'd have laid low for a month or so. Maybe I would have traveled and later would have come back to a different casino on the strip. Like I said, I don't have much of a plan."

"But that much money, you could buy a house or start a business or something. You could do anything."

"I am doing something," Jamie said as he pulled into the bank and put the car in park. "I'm getting you to New Hampshire."

"And I'm going to the bank, but I'm not asking you why," Trixie teased, raising her fingers up and crossing them over her heart.

"Good," he reached into the bag behind him and grabbed a stack of bills. "That's twelve thousand dollars. Create an account and deposit it."

"I'm supposed to walk in there with this giant stack of money like it's no big deal? What if they want to know where I got it?"

"Have you been to a bank before? They don't ask those types of questions. Just create the account. Deposit the money, and let me have the account information so I can set up what I need."

"You got it," Trixie said. "Hey Maisie, you're awake. Do you want to come into the bank with Mommy? I bet they have lollipops."

"Sure," Maisie sang as she unclipped her car seat buckles and looked thrilled to be released from the contraption.

Jamie watched the two of them disappear into the glass doors of the bank and took the opportunity to check the missed calls. Travis had been trying to reach him for weeks, and he'd just kept blowing him off. The man was relentless in his concern for Jamie. It had started years before when he took him in as a troubled foster kid, and it never stopped; it had only grown actually.

But Travis had finally found something that made him smile, and Jamie refused to be the person to ruin that for him. Taking off was his gift to Travis. Happiness was more balanced without him in the equation. It was hard though, because he knew Travis would be proud of what he was doing right now.

About twenty minutes later Trixie and Maisie came hopping out of the bank. The little girl's curls were bouncing up and down as she clutched a fistful of lollipops.

"You made out pretty well," Jamie said. He stepped out of the car and counted all the treats in her hand. She looked as excited as Trixie had when she heard how much money Jamie had won at the casino.

"Miss Tammy kept telling me to take another one and another one." Maisie wiggled into her seat as Jamie fastened the buckles. "Do you like green?" she asked, holding a lollipop right up to his nose. He nodded his head and smiled.

"Then you should take this one. It says thank you," she explained and pressed the pop against his nose again.

"It does?" he asked, making a silly face and crossing his eyes so he could look down at the gift. A laugh exploded from her belly.

"Yes," she breathed out between giggles. "I like living in your car better than where we lived before. I want to stay forever."

"Oh Maisie," Trixie interrupted, but Jamie waved her off.

"You're going somewhere even better. You're going to get a brand new place with your mom, and it's going to be way better than this car."

"Will you be there?" she asked, knitting her tiny brows nervously.

"Don't worry about that Maisie," Jamie said, tousling her hair. "Just worry about how many lollipops you can eat. We're going to be making a bunch of stops, and maybe we'll mini golf or do something else for fun."

When Jamie sunk into the front seat he could feel Trixie's eyes on him. In his peripheral vision he could see her opening her mouth to speak and then closing it again.

"The next hotel is probably going to be a dive," Jamie announced, desperate to change the subject.

"It doesn't matter," Trixie assured him. "I'd sleep on the cold hard dirt to keep her safe."

"She's safe," Jamie said with conviction. "Nothing is going to happen to either of you." He reached across and patted her knee. Before he could pull his hand back she grabbed it and laced her fingers between his.

"You're a good man, Jamie," she whispered and pulled his hand up and kissed his knuckles. "You're a very good man."

He thought about making a case for why she was wrong. He had a list of good reasons why he was a piece-of-crap deadbeat jerk. He could call character witnesses to back up his claims of douchebaggery. But instead he stayed quiet. Let her think the best of him if she wanted to. In a few days they'd part ways, and it wouldn't matter anyway. Maybe it would be nice to have one human on this planet thinking he was worth something—even if it weren't true.

CHAPTER SIX

The hotel was, in fact, a dive and they only had one room with one bed available. Jamie had insisted he'd crash on the floor but that was before he'd seen the shag carpet that looked more like a used towel.

"There is no way you're crashing on that nasty thing. You'll wake up with pink eye," Trixie said, lifting up her feet one at a time and looking like she half expected to be stuck to the floor.

"Then maybe just let me get a few hours of sleep and instead of crashing here overnight we just drive through the night again," Jamie suggested.

"No, we said we'd take an actual night of sleep here. You can't keep going on these little catnaps, and I'm not great at driving a stick, as you have pointed out. You need a full night's sleep."

"Well, I'll go and sleep out in the car then," Jamie said as he placed Maisie down on the bed with the two dolls he'd bought her at the last stop.

"We've shopped, we've eaten, and the sun is going down,"

Trixie said as they both watched Maisie let out a giant yawn. "Let's just get some sleep."

"All of us in the bed?" Jamie asked, making a face that showed how bad of an idea he thought that was.

"I'll put Maisie on the end. I'll take the middle. We've been sitting just as close in the car for the last couple of days. I think we can handle one night's sleep in the same bed."

"Slumber party," Maisie squealed.

Jamie rolled his eyes and clicked the light off as the girls settled into the bed. "I'm going to go grab some other stuff out of the car. I'll be back in a few."

"You going to have a smoke?" Trixie asked, winking at him.

"Maybe," he laughed.

"You haven't been smoking this whole trip. I thought for sure you'd have grabbed another pack of smokes at the last stop."

"It's not good for her," Jamie said, pointing with his chin over at Maisie, who was snuggling her dolls and looking ready for sleep. He slipped out the door and into the silence of the night.

After he'd snubbed out the cigarette against the sole of his shoe he walked quietly back into the hotel room. The lights were all off, and he could hear Maisie's soft rhythmic snoring.

"You sure about this," he whispered to Trixie as he stood, reluctant to move at the side of the bed.

"It's just sleep, Jamie. We need to sleep." She moved closer to her daughter and patted the bed for him to get in.

"He slid out of his boots and belt but opted to keep his jeans and shirt on. Trixie's skin was intoxicatingly soft and the less of it that touched his body right now the better.

Sleep was too hard to fight anyway. Trixie had been right. He was exhausted. Within a few minutes he was out cold.

A couple hours later, sometime around eleven, the sound of an unfamiliar ringing phone woke him. Trixie was in his arms, curled against his body. She too jumped at the foreign sound. They broke their twisted bodies apart quickly, and he hopped to his feet, looking to find the noise and silence it before it woke Maisie up.

"It's the cell you gave me. Who would have that number?" Trixie asked in a raspy whisper, pointing to the small table where she'd left the phone. He tossed it over to her.

"Hello?" she asked cautiously.

"Beatrix Aurula?" the woman's voice asked, and she froze at the thought of someone using her full name and calling her on a phone no one should know she has.

"Who is this?" she asked, quickly covering her mouth as if she might vomit.

"I'm breaking a lot of rules right now." The woman's voice was low and shaky. "This is Tammy from the bank today. I helped set up your account."

"Yes," Trixie said, still wondering if this was some kind of dream.

"A few hours after you and your daughter left a man called the bank and had a lot of questions about you. He claimed to be with the police back in Nevada. He wanted a description of you and asked if you were with anyone else. At first I thought maybe he was investigating some kind of crime. But then it became pretty clear by his questions that he was looking for you and wanting to know where you were headed."

"What did you tell him?" she asked desperately.

"He wasn't a cop was he?" Tammy asked.

"No, he's my ex and..."

"I spent three years with a man like that," Tammy explained. "I could tell something wasn't right about his questions. I didn't tell him anything. I asked for his badge number, and he didn't provide one. I told him to send the local police in if he wanted more information, and they could speak with the manager. He called me a few choice names and hung up. Then for the next hour he kept calling back, and I kept telling him the same thing. He told me he would just come out and find you himself."

"No," Trixie said, her eyes filling with tears. Jamie looked on, hearing bits and pieces of the conversation, enough to understand what was going on.

"I really shouldn't be telling you any of this. I'm not allowed to use the phone number you have on your account to contact you for something like this. But I just couldn't in good conscience keep this from you. That sweet little girl of yours, she was all I could think about."

"Thank you, Tammy. Thank you for warning me. Will he be able to get any information off the account if he shows up there in person?"

"Not without a legal document saying he or the police have the right to," Tammy explained. "Like I said I really shouldn't be getting involved in this at all."

"I know," Trixie said. "I hear what you're saying, and I can't thank you enough."

The line disconnected and Trixie stood frozen, staring over at her sleeping daughter who hadn't stirred a bit.

"We need to go now," Trixie said, a quake in her voice. "I'll pack stuff up and you go start the car."

"We're fine here, Trixie. So he knows you were at a bank a couple hours west of here. He's not going to find you tonight." Jamie made a move to touch her but she pulled away, shoving clothes into her bag.

"He would have hopped a flight. He's on his way out here. We need to get back on the road. I don't know what I was thinking. Of course he's looking for me. Eli will stop at nothing to show he's in control. Leaving was like a slap in the face to him. This was stupid."

"Trix, just sit down and take a breath," Jamie pleaded, trying to take the tote bag from her.

"Why did you make me open up that account? Why couldn't you do that yourself?" Tears blurred her angry glare, and that was the only thing keeping Jamie from flipping out on her. A crying woman got him every time.

"Let's get back on the road if that's what you want," Jamie offered, taking his keys from the nightstand.

"I want to Jamie, I really just think," she looked over at Maisie as she started to rustle beneath the blanket. "We need to Jamie." Her voice cracked with emotion, and she covered her mouth to quiet the sobs.

"We'll go now," Jamie assured her, pulling her into his arms. He whispered softly into her hair. "We'll go."

CHAPTER SEVEN

The cell phone in Trixie's hand rang, and out of instinct she threw it to the floor of the car. Jamie laughed and then remembered how raw her fear was.

"Is it that Tammy lady calling again?" Jamie asked, urging her to pick it up. "We haven't heard anything in over a day. We're only a few hundred miles from New Hampshire. It's probably nothing."

Jamie put his hand out and gestured for her to hand it over. She gave him the phone with a trembling hand.

"Hello?" he said in firmly.

"Where is Trixie?" a gravelly voice demanded. "Put her on the phone right now."

"You've got the wrong number dude," Jamie said and disconnected the call.

"Was it him?" she asked, clutching her chest.

"Was that Eli?" Maisie asked, peering back and forth between Jamie and her mother. "I thought you said he was all gone."

"He is all gone," Jamie insisted. "That wasn't him." He

lifted his knee to the steering wheel and used his hands to take the lid off the soda he got at the last drive thru. He submerged the phone then threw the cup out the window.

"How did he get the number?" she whispered, making sure Maisie was back to playing with her dolls.

"It doesn't matter. He won't get the next one." Jamie rolled his aching neck and yawned. He'd been pushing his body to the breaking point in a rush to get them to the east coast. Trixie had been on edge since Tammy had tipped her off about Eli. The car was painfully quiet for hours on end. She was pulling away from him, and he wasn't sure why. When Trixie pretended to sleep, Jamie could see the tears trickling down her cheeks. He just wanted to get her to New Hampshire, but he was so damn tired.

"You need to sleep. Let's stop somewhere," Trixie said. Jamie could hear the reluctance in her voice. Every time the wheels of the car slowed to a stop he could see the way her shoulders tensed up and her breath quicken. She was telling him to stop, but she didn't mean it.

"I can make it a little farther," he said, rubbing at his eyes.

"No, just pull over. There's a rest stop in a few miles. You can nap a little while Maisie and I go for a walk or eat some snacks or something." There was rigidness in her back that put Jamie on edge. Her eyes were like a wild horse, ready to bolt at any sign of trouble.

"I guess I could use a quick power nap," he agreed, not wanting to argue with someone who looked ready to snap.

Sleeping in a reclined seat in a car wasn't comfortable, but Jamie knew if he was going to push through the remainder of this trip and get Maisie and Trixie to New Hampshire he'd have to sleep. When they were settled in the rest stop parking lot he took one last look at Maisie and Trixie running in the field and then pulled his baseball cap down over his eyes.

A tap on the window woke him, and he wasn't sure if it had been five minutes or five hours since he'd dozed off. He popped up and tipped his hat back, trying to get his bearings.

"Can I talk to you for a minute?" Trixie asked, her lips pressed together firmly as though she was trying to hold her words back.

"Why?" That one word covered a lot of questions. Why are you waking me up? Why do you want to talk to me outside the car? Why do you look like you're ready to flip the hell out?

"Maisie, honey, you climb in and watch a show. I want to talk to Jamie for a bit." She opened the car door and unrolled the window. "We'll be right here."

"What's going on, Trix?" Jamie asked, still feeling like he could have used more sleep. Trixie was being cryptic, and he was feeling grumpy as hell now. It was not a great combination.

"When Maisie's dad died I ran right into Eli's arms. I really thought he was the answer to all my prayers. He was so willing to help and support us. I thought he was such a good man."

"So you screwed up," Jamie grumbled, still trying to figure out where this conversation was going.

"Yeah, I did." She laughed, sounding annoyed. "I needed someone because I've always been so damn convinced I can't make it on my own. But when you need someone so much you get dependent, it leaves you vulnerable. I can't afford that with Maisie around. I can't make the mistake I made with Eli again."

"I don't have a clue what you're talking about right now, Trixie," Jamie grunted. "I'm still kind of foggy, so if you could explain this to me we can save some time and get back on the road. I need a cup of coffee."

"Why are you sending fifteen hundred dollars a month to Sunny Creek Mental Institution in California?" She blurted out the words so quickly he almost didn't hear them correctly. If not for the very familiar name of the facility she mentioned he might have had her repeat herself.

"What did you do?" he asked, his nostrils flaring and his blood boiling.

"I had to know why you couldn't just open the bank account yourself. My job is to protect Maisie, and I need you to tell me why you're sending that money to a mental institution." Her hands were perched high on her hips, and her eyes were filled with fire.

"We had a deal Trixie, a damn fair deal," he barked. "All you had to do was stay out of my business, and I hand you a brand new life for you and your daughter. Why would you screw that up?"

"Because you're in that life right now, and I don't want to wake up and find you're no better than Eli. I have a responsibility to Maisie."

"Glad you finally have the brains in your head to realize you have a job to do. Congratulations on waking up and figuring out the people you let in your life shouldn't be deadbeats. It only took you four years." Jamie started backing away from her, not sure where he was heading. He just wanted distance, and he knew she wouldn't follow him if it meant leaving Maisie in the car.

"Jamie, please wait. If you tell me, if you can just let me know more about who you are, then we can work this out," Trixie begged, chasing him for a few steps and then stopping abruptly as though she was tethered by an invisible leash to the car.

"I don't owe you any explanation. I couldn't have been any clearer. My past is none of your damn business. If you didn't like the deal, you had a chance to speak up. All of the sudden you think I'm like Eli?"

"No," she cried. "I know you're not like Eli. You're a good man. I just don't want to go in blind. I want to know you."

"Why? You're only going to *know me* for a few more days. Who gives a shit if you get a look at all my scars? It won't even matter once I'm gone." He threw his hands up and glared angrily at her.

"Maybe I don't want you to go," Trixie said, averting her eyes, overcome by her own honesty.

He wanted to tell her she was being stupid. He'd very clearly explained to her what his life was going to be, once this was over. He laid out what he expected from her in return, and yet she was acting as though she'd never heard him at all. But instead he did what he said he would do.

"There's a car dealership off the highway about three miles back. We'll go there and pick you up something used but reliable. I'll give you guys the cash you need in New Hampshire, and we'll part ways."

"No Jamie, please don't say that. I'm sorry I broke my promise. I didn't mean to upset you, but don't take this out on Maisie. If you go now she'll be devastated. I wasn't trying to push you away. It was the complete opposite of that. I'm scared and confused, and I was trying to understand you."

"I was always leaving, Trixie. There was no scenario where I was going to live happily ever after with you and Maisie on some mountain. Don't make me out to be the bad guy. You should have let her know all along how this was going to end. That's not on me." Jamie threw his hands out as though he was passing the blame back to her like a hot potato.

"Fine, it's me. I was wrong, but that doesn't change anything. She's still about to be in a new place with all new people, and she's going to want you there. At least for a little while. Is that so wrong?"

"When I was her age I already knew damn well we don't always get what we want. Maybe this'll be a good lesson for her. Now, let's get you a car and finish this." Jamie marched to his car and flung the door open. Turning the engine over, he pumped the gas and revved the motor. Trixie stood there, shaking her head and whispering to herself.

Finally conceding, she marched around the front of the car and sank into the passenger seat. "I thought there was something here, Jamie; I wanted there to be. I hoped to know more about you."

"You wanted there to be something here, Trixie. Dreaming up some happy ending isn't going to give you what you're looking for in life. You've got a shot at starting fresh with your daughter. You should find a way to do that on your own two feet. You're a mom—act like one."

That was the headshot. If everything else they'd been lobbing at each other had banged her up and bruised her, that last sentence was enough to end her. She closed her mouth, gritted her teeth, and stared out the passenger window. He didn't want to be liked right now. That was complicated and required more personal connection than he was interested in, especially with a pair like Trixie and Maisie. So what if she was pissed at him, and they had to part ways like this; it was probably for the best. Nothing made a goodbye easier than anger.

CHAPTER EIGHT

"I want to ride in Jamie's car," Maisie insisted, stomping her foot against the asphalt of the car dealership.

"You can't," Trixie replied curtly, snatching her daughter's hand. "He's leaving. You and Mommy are going on to our new town like we talked about."

"I want Jamie," Maisie protested, but stopped abruptly when her mother gave her a rarely used, but wildly effective, death stare.

"That's just how things are Maisie. We've got a lot to look forward to, so let's just focus on that. Now sit in the car while I get our stuff and switch your seat over." Maisie shuffled her feet toward the silver nondescript car that would surely last another hundred thousand miles. Reliable. Maybe the first thing in Trixie's life that actually was.

Jamie cleared his throat and helped take some of the bags out of his trunk. "Right here is the address of an apartment you can stay in. It's small but the woman said she'd take cash. It's walking distance to the school and has lots of restaurants in the area if you want to waitress. You'll have enough cash to not worry about that for a little while though. I've got a guy who's going to mail you some new paperwork: birth certificates and stuff for both of you. Until then grab some prepaid credit cards and a cell phone. That should get you by until then." Jamie handed Trixie a piece of paper with all the information she would need.

"I want to tell you so badly to go to hell. If I could I would crumple up this paper and throw it in your face. But I can't. I've screwed my life over so bad I can't even turn this down on principle. I'd have nothing. I don't even have the ability to turn down the help of someone I'm pissed at. That's a tough pill to swallow, but like you pointed out, it's my own fault. So it's important for you to know if it was within my power I'd walk away from you right now and never look back."

Jamie gnawed at the inside of his lip and squinted against the sun beating down on his face. "I don't know what you want me to say," he admitted with a shrug. "I hope it works out for you two. It's not that I don't want you to be happy."

"I have to know . . ." Trixie sang out, "weren't you having a good time? I know we were crammed in a car, and you did all the driving. Maisie can be a chatterbox sometimes. But when it was quiet, when the windows were down, didn't it seem kind of right? If so, what was so bad about opening up a little bit?"

Jamie was sorry she was still trying so hard. Most people would have given up on him by now. "You're going to lose the light," he replied flatly and dropped his eyes down to his shoes, kicking at some loose gravel. "When you get your new phone number shoot me a text. If anything goes wrong, let me know." He jingled his car keys around in his hand and then tapped on the car window. "Hey kiddo, be good for your mommy. You're going to love the mountains."

"When are you going to come visit?" Maisie asked, her lip quivering into a pout.

"You'll start getting excited about seeing the leaves change in a few months and sledding in the snow. I'll be around. Keep an eye on the mail too." He reached in the window and gave her a high five.

"She'll be fine," Trixie said coolly as she slammed the trunk closed.

"So will you," Jamie assured her as he nodded goodbye. Her car sped out of the lot and disappeared down the road toward the highway. He was free. No one was looking to him for help. No one was asking questions about his past. With a trunkful of money he could go do whatever he wanted now. He could go anywhere in the world. So why did he want to follow them?

CHAPTER NINE

"Damn faucet," Trixie hissed as she tried to tighten the knob to make the incessant dripping noise stop.

"No bad words, Mommy," Maisie scolded as she colored the unicorn in her notebook. It had been twenty-one days in this apartment, and Trixie still felt like she hadn't accomplished anything. There had been a small amount of furniture already in it. Enough to make them comfortable for a short time until they could buy their own things. She'd done some food shopping, but every time she went to cook she realized what was missing from the kitchen. No strainer for the pasta. No can opener for the sauce. There were dozens of emergency trips to the corner store, and she was thoroughly frazzled. But she was surviving. There were even a few moments of the day when she didn't look over her shoulder, expecting to see Eli there. Or worse, hoping to see Jamie.

"We need to go to the hardware store," Trixie said, realizing she couldn't fix this stupid faucet with a butter knife and a pair of scissors.

"Why don't you call Eli?" Maisie asked as she slid into her shoes and adjusted the barrette in her hair.

"What?" Trixie asked, crumpling her face as if she must have heard the little girl wrong. "Why?"

"He fixes things, Mommy," she replied simply. "You don't know how to fix things."

"Maybe I don't," Trixie said, crouching down and clutching her daughter's tiny shoulders. "This thing might never stop dripping, but I'd rather have that problem than call someone who was not nice to us. Do you understand that? It's not worth being with someone mean just because things are hard without them. We don't need Eli or people like him."

The mail slot in the door squeaked open and a flurry of junk mail tumbled to the floor. Maisie ran toward it with a buzz of excitement.

"Look, Mommy, there's a new one," she squealed as she plucked the postcard off the floor. "It's Silky Bear. Where is he this time?"

Trixie peered down at the postcard and smiled. It was clearly doctored by some computer program, but her daughter couldn't tell the toy wasn't the original Silky Bear, and he wasn't actually standing at the edge of the Grand Canyon. "Oh he looks like he's having a lot of fun on his trip," Trixie explained. "This is the Grand Canyon. It's so big. I bet he's staying there a whole week."

"I miss him," Maisie said, hugging the postcard to her chest.

"I miss him too," Trixie sighed, talking about the sender rather than the star of the pictures. "Come on sweet girl. Let's go buy some tools. I know if we put our minds to it, we can figure this out."

The walk to the hardware store brought Trixie peace. The small street was lined with trees, whose leaves were rustling in the breeze. Birds were chirping and squirrels were scurrying along. This place was the complete opposite of Vegas, and that was exactly what she was looking for. Jamie had picked the perfect spot for them.

When she pulled open the hardware store's door Maisie clapped at the jingling bell that rang out overhead.

"Hello there, Miss Maisie." Dwayne smiled and waved. Before meeting Dwayne, Trixie had never actually seen a grown man wearing overalls. His big belly pushed them to the point of nearly bursting. Those pants were working hard.

"Hello Mr. Dwayne," she chirped back. "Our sink is going drip, drip, drip, and my mommy said she's going to go crazy if it doesn't stop."

"Oh, that's a pain," Mr. Dwayne replied, tucking his thumbs into the straps of his overalls. "I can come by and fix that up in a jiff. Let me call Rocky and have him cover the store for me."

"No," Maisie said, shaking the curls on her head before Trixie could jump in and decline the offer herself. "My mommy needs to fix it. We don't need anyone's help, because some people are bad, and we need to do things by ourselves, right Mommy?" She tipped her head back and blinked quickly up at her mom.

"I . . . um . . . well that's not exactly it but—"

"I think it's a great idea," Dwayne replied with a hearty chuckle. "You two seem plenty capable of fixing a leaky faucet. Let me get you what you need, and if you're interested I can give you a quick lesson."

"That would be great," Trixie replied gratefully. She tried to cool the burning embarrassment in her cheeks.

"Your mommy is sure doing right by you," Dwayne said as he turned his back and started looking for the tools she'd need. "It's good to be able to take care of yourself."

"Because of the mean Eli's," Maisie agreed.

"Maisie honey, please don't."

"Would you like a lollipop, Miss Maisie?" Dwayne asked, plucking one from behind the counter, tearing off the wrapper and handing it over. Sometimes there was no better plug in the world than a lollipop. "I've got crayons out over there." He pointed at the small card table in the corner. "Will you draw me another rainbow?"

Without another word she hopped over to the table and got right to work, plucking just the right colors out of a small metal bin.

"I'm sorry about that, Dwayne. There are days I'm not sure what to tell her and what to keep from her. I don't want her to think everyone in the world is bad, but I don't want her believing everyone deserves her trust either. I don't know the answer."

"Nobody does, Miss Trixie," Dwayne laughed. "You and Maisie, maybe you had a tougher road but that question you're asking yourself right now, it's what we all ask ourselves as parents. I'm watching my own kids go through it with my grandkids. It's a scary world, and we try to prepare them the best we can."

"I don't want to let her down anymore," Trixie said, wiping away a single runaway tear.

"Start with the faucet," Dwayne said, flashing his slightly gapped teeth at her. "The rest will fall into place. Tower Falls is a great town. We're small, but we're mighty. Whatever you've got behind you, let it stay there. Start fresh here, and she'll do just fine. Both of you will."

"Eli," she croaked out. "I don't know if he'll ever let us go. I think he might always look for us. I did that. I brought that on us. She deserves more than the danger that comes with my bad choices."

"You're going to be fine," Dwayne said, patting her hand. "You might want to learn to do all these things alone. You may think you've got to be on your own two feet, and that's good. She should see that. But as long as you live in this town you won't be alone. Let him come. Let him try. You and Maisie are one of us now. We stand together."

"Thanks Dwayne," Trixie said, clearing her throat, trying to gain her composure.

"So tell me more about this faucet; is it a standard or a spray hose head?" He pushed his hands into the huge pockets of his overalls and listened intently. He was right. All she needed to do was start with the faucet. One day at a time. One step at a time she'd show her daughter they could survive on their own. Being alone didn't make you hopeless or helpless. It could make you strong.

CHAPTER TEN

"Order up," the cook called from behind the deli counter as he tapped his bell. Trixie hopped up from the booth where she was sitting with Maisie and went to retrieve the plate.

"Keep working on your letters," she said as she pulled her apron back on. Working in a small breakfast place didn't pay at all like being a Vegas cocktail waitress did, but no one here pawed her. Her body wasn't hanging out of her clothes. She didn't judge the women she worked with. Many were some of the best people she'd ever met. Seeing her daughter beam with pride when she balanced all those plates, warmed her heart in a way a big tip never could.

"Can I get you guys anything else?" she asked the four men at a table who'd already started digging into their food. She knew their names and that they were loggers because they came in every single morning and ordered the same thing. Those heaps of eggs and bacon were the fuel that would carry them through an almost impossible, physically strenuous day.

"I'll take a refill," Bob said, gulping down the last of his black coffee. "And order Maisie a pink sprinkled donut. Make sure you put it on our bill."

"Yeah," Maisie said, standing up excitedly in the booth.

"Sit down young lady," Trixie ordered, and she quickly obeyed. "She heard you, so there's no telling her no now." Her smile let them know not only did she not mind her daughter getting the treat, she was grateful.

"Thank you, Bob," Maisie called as she hurried and scribbled on the paper. "I'm making you something."

"Can't wait, kiddo," Bob laughed. "I'll hang it up in the truck."

"Hey, Trix," one of the men said, his face washing white as though he'd just seen a ghost. "You might want to see this." He gestured at the television over the counter. "Turn that up."

She turned to see a picture of her and Maisie on the screen. Pictures that used to sit on the mantle in the house she shared with Eli.

The news anchor spoke in a solemn tone as he explained the story. "The woman and her daughter have been missing for over a month, and her fiancé is speaking out asking for the public's help. Eli Strauss, the son of United States Senator Clive Strauss spoke with reporters yesterday. He states that the woman, Beatrix Aurula, who goes by Trixie, and her daughter, Maisie Aurula, went missing in May. He reported it to the police, but no Amber Alert was issued because there was no sign of foul play or indication they had been taken against their will. Now as more time has passed, and they've had no luck locating the woman and her daughter, Strauss is urging the public to help. He believes they may be traveling with a man who has a history of crime and possibly mental illness."

The frame switched quickly away from the picture of her and Maisie, to a clip of Eli. He was dressed in a pressed shirt, his face was clean-shaven and his eyes were rimmed as though he'd been crying. "I'm asking everyone to please help me bring my family home. They are my whole life, and not knowing where they are is killing me. Trixie, honey, if you can hear me please find a way to call home. Find a way to reach me, and I promise I will come for you. I will bring you home no matter what."

The screen cut back to the reporter, who continued the story. "Strauss and his family are offering a twenty thousand dollar reward for any tips on the whereabouts of his fiancée and her daughter. We reached out to the police for a statement, and at this time we are still waiting to hear from them. Here is the hotline the Strauss family has set up for any information you may have on the whereabouts of the missing woman and her daughter."

Trixie backed up until she nearly fell into Bob's lap, catching herself on the edge of the booth. "We need to go," she said breathlessly. She tried to untie her apron but couldn't get her shaking hands to free the knot.

"That bastard," Bob said, standing and clicking the television off. "No one here is going to say anything Trix." He tried to assure her. "It could be a million dollars and no one would call that hotline. You guys are safe here."

"He's not going to stop," she whispered and finally was free of her apron. "I don't think there is anywhere we can go that he couldn't find us." She ran her hands through her hair and paced, trying to think of a plan.

"Call the police," Bob suggested. "Tell them you aren't under any duress, and you left on your own free will. You don't even have to tell them why if you're afraid of retribution from him. But at least it would make this whole *help from the public* thing go away."

"Maybe," she agreed, shaking her head at that logical plan. "Maybe that's what I'll do."

"This is a small town, Trixie," Bob reminded her. "People don't just pass through this way or show up without some good reason. If he or someone else comes here looking for you, they won't get far. I can call the sheriff and put him on alert. We only have the four cops in town, but all of them can be on the lookout too. They know you, they know why you're here."

"Twenty thousand dollars," she said, knitting her brows together. "People here need that kind of money. I wouldn't blame them if they called the hotline. How could I ask them not to?"

"You don't have to ask," Bob assured her. "We'll spread the word and make sure everyone knows the real story. You keep going on like nothing changed. Get that little girl her sprinkle donut and keep moving forward."

She shook her head in agreement, even though she wasn't sure she'd be able to make her legs move. Her mind had gone through plenty of ways Eli might track her down, but this was not one of them. His father's clout was changing the game, and she had to be ready for anything now. If the last couple months had been about being independent and strong, this would be her time to prove it. She just wasn't quite sure how yet.

CHAPTER ELEVEN

"I like your haircut, Mommy," Maisie said, reaching up and patting her mother's head. Trixie laughed because she knew it was a lie. No one could like the haircut she'd gotten. The only point of it was to change the way she looked in the picture the news kept flashing everywhere. She'd kept the television off so Maisie didn't know what was happening. Instead she watched the news ticker on her phone for any new updates.

It had been relatively quiet for the last twenty-four hours, but as she clicked on the screen she could tell something had changed.

"Honey, go in my room and put on your cartoons," Trixie said, hustling her out of the room as she turned on the television. The familiar local reporter was reading from a piece of paper she'd just been handed.

"We have reports the woman, Beatrix Aurula, from Nevada, has been spotted in the small town of Tower Falls in New Hampshire. Her fiancé, Eli Strauss, has already released a statement. He will personally go and follow every lead he receives that is deemed viable. He could not be reached for comment, but a spokesperson for his family stated he was already en route to our area."

Trixie's knees wobbled and then quit altogether, buckling and sending her down to a praying position. He was coming. Sure she had the support of the whole town. But she'd been with Eli long enough to know it wouldn't matter. One way or another he'd get what he wanted. She knew soon enough he'd be saying, "If I can't have you, no one can."

"Baby," she called out to Maisie, "we need to go. Grab the bags we've packed." There were certain skills that came from running away from your own life. You kept the car full of gas no matter how many times you had to stop and fill it up in a week. Bags ready to leave in an instance were tucked under her bed. Maisie had been prepped for what it might mean to leave in a hurry.

"Why?" Maisie asked, shuffling out of her room, looking like she might burst into tears. "I don't want to leave here."

"We talked about this, Maisie," Trixie said angrily. "You know we have to put our safety before anything else."

"I'm not going," she said, folding her arms across her chest and planting her feet as though it might keep her mom from being able to move her.

"Stop acting like a baby. You're four years old." The words flew from her mouth, and all she could punctuate them with was a tiny laugh. "You're four years old," she repeated. "You're acting like a four-year-old." What a silly thing to say. Her daughter was still a baby, and she had every right to act like one.

Maisie crumpled into tears and sank to the floor. Trixie raced toward her and took her curled up body into her lap and rocked her. "I'm sorry, honey. You are four years old. You're not supposed to understand any of this. You're supposed to have roots, and I keep yanking them out of the ground just as you start to settle in. It's not fair."

"So we can stay?" Maisie asked, peeking up at her mother from under her wet eyelashes. Having to dash that hopefulness in her child's eyes hurt her more than any physical pain Eli had ever inflicted.

"We can't," she apologized and squeezed her daughter as tight as she could. "I'm so sorry you have to go through this. It's Mommy's fault. But we still have to get our bags and go."

"Can we say goodbye?" Maisie pleaded. It was a small request, considering how much they were about to give up.

"We can," Trixie agreed reluctantly. "It'll have to be quick though."

After twenty minutes of grabbing bags, negotiating over what had to stay behind and what could come with them, they were down on the street, deciding who to say goodbye to first.

Her phone chirped with an update, and she pulled it up quickly. There on her screen was a photo of Jamie, claiming he might be responsible for the disappearance of her and Maisie. "No," she cried out.

"What's wrong?" Maisie asked, looking scared.

"Nothing, it's fine. We just need to say goodbye and get on the road. Everything will be fine. We've got the car packed, full of gas, and Mommy has a plan. You have nothing to worry about."

"Sounds like you have everything under control," a familiar voice said over her shoulder. She nearly jumped out of her skin, clutching Maisie's hand so tightly her daughter yelped.

"Jamie," Maisie called out, wiggling free and running toward him. "Are you here to help us?"

"It looks like your mom has it all taken care of, but I might tag along with you. I'm interested to know what her plan is. I bet it'll be great." Jamie smiled over at Trixie as he lifted Maisie up and put her on his shoulders.

"Did you see the news? They have your picture up and your name. They're saying you have something to do with this. I should have called the police and told them I left on my own. I didn't have the courage, and now you could be in trouble too. That's not what I wanted."

"I saw it." Jamie shrugged. "No big deal. I'm always in trouble. This is nothing new for me."

She shook her head as though something didn't compute. "Why are you here? I thought you'd be on a beach somewhere by now."

"I've been staying about a half hour from here. Every time I got in my car to get back on the road, I changed my mind." Jamie tickled Maisie's knee and sent her squirming.

"Why?" Trixie asked, praying he'd say something that spoke to her tired heart.

"Two reasons," was all he could muster as he turned his head and stared across the street as though there was something interesting there.

"Am I one?" Maisie asked, holding on to his hair and tugging it as she balanced herself on his shoulders.

"Maybe," he said, finally meeting Trixie's stare. "Maybe you are."

"Hey," a booming voice shouted from across the street as

a mob of people charged toward them. "Put her down you son of a bitch," Bob demanded and pulled the bat in his hand back threateningly.

"No," Trixie said, putting her body between Jamie and the parade of people looking ready to pull him limb from limb. "This is Jamie. He's the one who got us here. He's the one who saved us."

The momentum of the crowd coming their way took a long moment to stop. Some of the men weren't convinced until she pressed her hand to their chests and pleaded with them to calm down.

"He's the good guy," Maisie sang, hugging his head and kissing his hair. When most of the men seemed to relax, Jamie dropped Maisie down and extended his hand to them.

"Jamie, the good guy." He laughed, introducing himself with a chuckle. "Glad to see the girls aren't on their own here. Maybe I didn't need to come back after all."

"It looks like you did," Bob said, gesturing down to Maisie who had her arms wrapped around one of Jamie's legs.

"So what's the plan? You heard what just came across the news, right? He knows you're here. He's coming," Barb, a fellow waitress, said, looking to each of them for an answer.

"Canada," Trixie said confidently. "We just need to try to find a place to cross the border that won't raise any flags. There has to be something, right?"

"There is," Bob said. "My brother-in-law has a cabin and some land right on the line. He can get you across."

"I'm going to leave my car," Jamie said, tossing his keys to Bob. "They'll be looking for it, but not for your car, Trixie. Keep an eye on it for me, will you?"

"You're leaving your car?" Trixie asked, knowing exactly

how much Jamie loved that vehicle. It was sleek and fast, far more fun than the reliable car he'd bought for her.

"It's just a car," Jamie said. His phone started ringing relentlessly, and he switched it quickly to silent. "Let's get out of here. We should try to get across the border tonight, if we can."

A dozen hugs and well wishes later they were on the road. Just like the trek across the country, they fell into a rhythm that worked. Maisie was humming, Trixie fiddled with the radio, and Jamie drove with determination. "I've got the address for Bob's brother-in-law's cabin. We'll make good time."

Jamie's phone kept buzzing, and finally Trixie lifted it from the center console. "Who is Travis?" she asked. "I know you didn't want me knowing anything about you, but that was before. You came back. That was your choice. I don't want you to stonewall me."

"He's a guy who helped me out when I was in trouble. I was in the foster care system, and he took me in. For the last five years or so he's been, I don't know, like trying to watch out for me. Believe it or not, I'm not easy to get along with."

"So he's like a dad to you?" Trixie asked, watching the phone glow again. "If that's the case, you need to answer this call. He's likely seen the news, and he's going out of his mind with worry. Don't do that to him."

"You won't like the advice he gives us, trust me." Jamie took the phone from her but didn't make a move to answer it yet.

"If it were me," she said softly, "and I thought Maisie was in trouble, I'd go mad waiting to hear from her."

Jamie looked at her and rolled his eyes. "Hello," he said, looking annoyed as he answered the phone.

"Where the hell are you? Have you seen the news?" Travis blurted over the speakerphone. "You need to turn yourself in as soon as possible, and I'll call your lawyer. Don't make this any worse than it is."

"There's more to the story than the news is saying," Jamie explained.

"Of course there is," Travis shouted. "You obviously didn't kidnap some woman and her daughter so clear it up."

"Her ex is after her. He's got a lot of power and an axe to grind. I'm getting them out of the country. It's the only way they'll be safe."

"Oh Jamie," he heard Autumn say in the background. "I know it probably seems like that's the only option, but there are people who can help."

"I've got it under control," Jamie argued. "Trust me, they'll be fine."

"Jamie," Travis said very seriously, "I know this little girl reminds you of your own past, and you want to keep her safe. That's admirable. I respect the man you've become and what you're trying to do. But you need to come home. You can't do this alone, and you don't need to."

"I'm not sixteen anymore," Jamie barked back. "I have money; I have a car. I can do this differently than I did before."

"But you're not. You're doing exactly the same thing, and history will repeat itself. You believed you could keep everything under control, but you can't. What happens when you get pulled over, and they arrest you? Who will protect them then? Just come home. I can help you. You're right; you're not sixteen anymore. And you're not alone anymore either. Can you please trust me? Haven't I done enough for you over the years to prove I've got your back?"

Jamie dropped the phone lower. "I'll call you back in a few minutes. This isn't my decision to make."

Jamie looked over at Trixie and sighed. "I told you that would be his advice. He'd never think running was a good idea."

"You trust him?" Trixie asked, swallowing the lump in her throat. "Do you think he's right?"

"Travis is the most levelheaded and compassionate guy I know. How he's dealt with me over the years is a mystery to me. He's got to be up for sainthood by now. People like him. They listen to him. He's gotten me out of so many jams. He never gives up."

Trixie's mouth curled into a tiny smile. "I hope Maisie talks about me like that someday."

"I'm sure she will. Look what you're doing for her already. You're willing to do anything to keep her safe. That matters. The choice is yours now where you want to go. The only thing I'll say is, if there is a way to solve this without spending the rest of your life running, Travis will figure it out."

"I don't want her to have a lifetime full of goodbyes," Trixie said solemnly, peeking back at her daughter. "I want her to have a place she thinks of as home. Somewhere she can always return to no matter what."

Jamie pulled the car off to the side of the road and quickly turned around, heading the other way. "He'll be shocked to see us," Jamie admitted. "I'll be honest, when I have to make a choice like this, I almost always go the other way. I think I can fix things myself or I can outrun things."

"And how has that worked out for you?" she asked, reaching her hand over and touching his knuckles gently.

"It's a disaster." He let go of the steering wheel and took her hand in his. "But this will be different. This is all going to be fine. Travis will fix this."

CHAPTER TWELVE

Jamie knew exactly what to expect when they pulled into Autumn's driveway. Travis was out front, pacing around impatiently. Chuck Donahue's unmarked cop car was parked in the street, and he was probably in the house, sucking down a cup of black coffee.

When Jamie stepped out of the car Travis had a completely foreign look on his face. It was strange to think you could know a man for five years and he still had expressions you hadn't witnessed yet. It was pride mixed with relief. Autumn came around to Trixie's side of the car, offering a smile and a hand with her bag.

Travis, on the other hand, came straight up to Jamie and pulled him into a hug. Not something they'd done much of over the years. "I love you, kid," he said in a gravelly voice. "You made the right choice."

"I . . . uh," Jamie said awkwardly. "Yeah, me too."

"Wrap up the reunion," Chuck called from the doorway of Autumn's house, gesturing for them all to come in.

"Chuck's here to help. You're not in any trouble," Travis

assured Jamie with a hard pat on the back. "We're going to sort this out." He was smiling so wide Jamie had to shoot him a sideways glance to try to get him to rein it in a bit. "Sorry," Travis said, settling his face. "I just wasn't sure you were really coming."

"I'm here," Jamie said with a hint of attitude he didn't even really mean. It was a habit.

Jamie opened Maisie's door, unclipped her seat, and carried her inside. Her head was bobbing back and forth like a ragdoll as she slept on his shoulder.

"You can put her in one of the beds upstairs," Autumn whispered, and she followed him up to make sure he'd have everything he needed.

When he came back down everyone was silent and staring at him expectantly. "What?" he asked, looking down as though he might have spilled coffee all over him or something.

"So obviously I've seen the news, Jamie," Chuck said, sitting down on the couch and flipping a notebook open. "I figured I'd be getting a call from my buddy Travis to try to get you out of whatever trouble you've gotten into this time."

"It's not like that," Travis defended, even though he didn't really know the whole story yet.

"I've heard you say that so many times, brother," Chuck groaned. "We've been going round and round like this for five years, and if not for our friendship and the many times you bailed me out when I was young, Jamie would be in jail. But now is your chance; if there's another side to this story then let's hear it."

Travis opened his mouth to talk, but Chuck quieted him

by raising his hand. "I'd like to hear it from these two please," he said, gesturing at Trixie and Jamie.

Trixie cleared her throat and fiddled with the bracelet on her wrist. "I met Jamie while he was playing blackjack at the casino I worked at in Vegas. He was a regular, so I got to know him a little. I went outside with him while he was having a smoke, and my boyfriend showed up. He thought something more was going on, and he flipped."

"It's more than that," Jamie cut in. "He'd driven to the casino piss drunk with her daughter in the truck. He parked in some garage and left her to bake in the heat. She could have suffocated. Then he assaulted Trixie."

"Is there a report filed about the assault, child endangerment, DUI, anything?" Chuck jotted a few notes down and looked up at them expectantly.

"When we found Maisie I made the decision to leave," Trixie said, staring down at her shoes.

"I'd done well at the casino," Jamie explained. "I was pretty much finished in Vegas anyway and planned to move on. I offered her a ride out of town and some help getting back on her feet." Jamie looked over at Travis and Autumn, who were quietly beaming but quickly became serious again.

Chuck nodded his head as though he was following along. "Was there a history of abuse?" he asked, looking straight at Trixie, indicating she was the only one he wanted to hear from.

"Yes," she croaked out, looking embarrassed.

"What type? Physical, with many documented injuries?"

"Three cracked ribs," Trixie started. "A broken wrist. Three broken toes. Black eyes. Split lip. Stitches. Should I keep going?"

"No," Chuck said, waving her off. "How many times has he been arrested?"

"None, and that time wouldn't have been any different. His father is a U.S. Senator. Every time something happens, he swoops in and gets it taken care of before anything goes on record. DUIs and assault charges just disappear. That night, when I saw Maisie in the truck alone . . . it was so hot. I knew I had no other choice. He'd kill us someday, and no one was going to stop him. He still might."

Jamie moved toward Trixie and put a hand on her shoulder to steady her.

Chuck nodded again. "No one is going to kill anyone. You made the right choice by coming here rather than running. We've got this under control now."

"What's the plan?" Travis asked.

"I'm going to call the department in Nevada, and let them know you're here and you left on your own free will. I'll ask them to make a statement to public, and have Eli back off with this media storm he's creating."

"He'll come here," Trixie said urgently.

"It would be my pleasure to arrest him if he comes here with any intent to hurt you. I don't know his dad, and I don't give a crap who he is." Chuck closed the notebook and stood. "Let's not waste any time though. I'll get them on the phone."

Chuck stepped into the kitchen and made a quick call to his office, letting them know what he had planned. Once he had the go-ahead he was dialing with the speaker on so everyone could hear.

"Hello, this is Officer Chuck Donahue, badge number 2-04984 out of Waynesville, Connecticut. I'm calling in connection to the Beatrix Aurula case. She's here with me, and she'd like to make a statement."

"I'll transfer you to the task force," a nasally woman said.

"Task force?" Chuck asked, knitting his brows together.

"Yes, there is a federal task force that's been formed. You'll be speaking with Federal Marshal Joe Contenelli." The line went quiet, and the look on Chuck's face spoke volumes.

"This is Marshal Contenelli," a man said curtly and Chuck stood up a little straighter.

"Hello Marshal, my name is Officer Chuck Donahue. I'm out of a precinct in Connecticut, and I'm here with Beatrix Aurula. She's made a statement to me, and I'd like to pass the information along to you."

"That won't be necessary," he said tersely. "If you can keep her detained we'll have an escort bring her back to Nevada as soon as possible. She can give her statement here."

"She's not detained," Chuck explained, his cheeks growing red with sudden frustration. "As far as I know she hasn't committed any crime and isn't a danger to anyone. She came to me for assistance in clearing up the situation. I don't believe it's her desire to go back to Nevada. If you have a moment I can shed more light on this."

"We'll have an escort at your precinct in the morning. She can explain whatever she wants when she gets back here." Contenelli sounded distracted and uninterested in anything Chuck had to say.

"Again," Chuck reiterated, looking over at a shaking Trixie, "she has no desire to return to the state. There's no warrant issued for her, so I'm not following why you'd have her transported back there."

"There's no reason for you to have to follow what's going on. This is far above your pay grade, friend. Just keep her there, and we'll take care of it."

"I'd like you to speak with my captain," Chuck said, urgency in his voice. "I can connect your call to him now."

"Fine," the marshal said. "This is a federal investigation, you have no jurisdiction over the matter and these are my orders. She's coming back to Nevada. You can connect me to your captain now if you'd like so I can get the information on your precinct."

Chuck walked back into the kitchen, turning his back on everyone. Clicking some buttons on the screen of his phone he connected the call to his captain and hung up.

"What the hell was that?" Jamie shouted, but quieted when Autumn pointed to the ceiling, reminding him about a sleeping Maisie upstairs. "You need to do something."

"I . . . um," Chuck stuttered, "why would this be federal? If it is, there is nothing anyone around here is going to be able to do."

"We need a new plan," Travis said, trying to sound calm. Jamie's body language was screaming, and Travis was reacting to his cues.

Trixie tried to clear her throat enough to sound steady, but it didn't work. Her quaking voice betrayed her. "I can't go back to Nevada. I have no idea who they have in their corner. They could make any kind of accusation against me and take Maisie away."

"Let's get back on the road," Jamie said, clutching her hand. "We'll head for Mexico this time."

"No," Travis said, shooting to his feet. "You're not

running from this. I don't care how powerful this asshole thinks he is."

It was one of the first time Jamie heard Travis swear like that, and it took him back a bit. "I get what you're saying, Travis, but they're coming for her. None of your local connections are going to be able to help."

"I might have someone I can call," Autumn said, starting out meekly and then growing in confidence as she spoke. "My husband, Charlie, my late husband," she corrected. "He was a lawyer in a big firm in Greenwich. His partners are fierce, and I know they would do anything for me. They loved Charlie. I could call Roberta Silverstone. You'll need some kind of legal counsel."

"That's a great idea," Chuck chimed in. "I'm going to go in and meet with my captain face to face. I'll see if he can call in some favors of his own." Chuck looked down at his phone as it chirped with a text message. "It looks like ETA for these asshats from Nevada is ten tomorrow morning. You're expected to be at my precinct then."

"She's not going with them," Jamie said with a fire in his belly. "It'll be over my dead body. And theirs."

"Hopefully it won't come to that," Travis said, giving a nod to Chuck as he went out the front door.

He seemed to take everyone's ability to speak with him. They all stood in silence, glancing at each other helplessly. Finally Autumn got to her feet and spoke.

"I'll make dinner," she said, forcing cheerfulness. "I'm not much of a cook. How does everyone feel about peanut butter and jelly?"

"My favorite," Maisie called from the top of the stairs as

she slid on her backside all the way down. "You can leave the crusts on, I eat that now, too."

"Hey sweetheart," Trixie said, trying to compose herself. "This is Travis." She gestured over to him, and he crouched down, extending his hand for a shake. She turned it over and pulled it to her lips, kissing his knuckles the way a prince would. "Pleasure to me you," she sang. "You're Jamie's daddy?"

"Well," Travis corrected, bunching his face up as he tried to find the right explanation. "Jamie and I—"

"He said you help him when he's in trouble, and you always never leave him alone, even when he wants you to. He lived with you, and you took care of him. That makes you his daddy."

"Kid, come get your sandwich," Jamie grumbled, swooping in and picking her up before the conversation could get any more uncomfortable. Jamie and Travis were the stereotype of men who didn't share feelings. They did much better with grunts of cavemen communication. They'd managed to get by that way for years. Why stop now?

CHAPTER THIRTEEN

Roberta Silverstone's power suit was so firmly starched and perfectly fitted to her body it looked as though it could stand up on its own if she wasn't wearing it. Her slicked-back red hair was pulled into a tight bun, and the glossy lipstick she had on matched perfectly. Autumn had been right; one phone call and Roberta was there to help.

"I think I have a handle on the situation," Roberta said, her annunciation of each word accompanied by her raised hand halted all the chatter. "You're in a very interesting position, Trixie."

"It doesn't feel interesting," Trixie admitted. "It feels terrifying."

"So what are our options?" Jamie asked impatiently, pacing around Autumn's living room.

"Normally I would say we should call their bluff. There has been no warrant issued for her arrest. Eli Strauss has no legal claim to the child. These are likely just scare tactics. But," she said, dragging the word out, "his father Clive is a very powerful man. He sits on numerous committees, which make funding decisions for many sectors of the country. The favors he must have in his back pocket from earmarking money and swinging votes would be astounding."

"Meaning?" Jamie asked with a huff.

"If we challenge their right to detain or transport Trixie, they'll just create whatever we claim they don't have. I'm sure within a few hours they could have a warrant out for her arrest on some bogus charge and enough witnesses to back it up. What you need are character witnesses of your own. People who know what kind of mother you are and what kind of monster Eli is."

Trixie twisted the bracelet on her wrist and searched the room, looking like she'd love to bolt right now. "The problem with that is, I don't have anyone. It didn't happen all at once, but little by little I cut people out of my life to be with Eli. He didn't like me talking to my friends on the phone. I never socialized with the other waitresses at work."

Roberta looked disappointed but not ready to give up. "The account you gave of the night Eli drove drunk and put Maisie at risk mentioned some security workers. They sounded fairly familiar with your situation."

"They've pulled Eli off me plenty of times," Trixie said, lighting a little flicker of hope but quickly snuffing it out. "But they would be risking their jobs if they told their side of the story. Eli is untouchable, and they know it. They have all been silenced in one way or another over the years, and I couldn't ask them to give up everything for me."

"If they're under oath they'd have no choice. I could subpoena them for a statement about that night and any other instances of threats or abuse they witnessed. Now how about your daughter?" Roberta leaned in closer, looking like she was finally getting somewhere.

"What about her?" Trixie asked defensively.

"She must have witnessed the abuse as well. Did he ever hit her? If she were on the stand could she recall what it was like to be trapped in that hot car?" Roberta was speaking so matter-of-factly it was as if she was asking for Trixie's favorite color.

"He never touched her," Trixie said quickly as though it was the most important distinction she could make. "I'm sorry to say she has seen him hit me. I'm not sure I want to put her through the process of having to talk about it though."

"She might be the most powerful witness you could have," Roberta said, typing away at her keyboard and not even sparing Trixie a glance.

Roberta was plowing forward while Trixie was clearly feeling like things were suddenly moving too fast. Travis tried to alleviate the tension that was building. "What exactly are you proposing?"

Roberta kept typing as she spoke. "Let's get everyone we can on record. If these guys are going to come at you hard the best thing you can do is strike first." She balled her hand into a fist as though it were some kind of rallying cry.

"How?" Trixie asked, feeling her stomach swirl with terror. She'd spent so many years learning how to not provoke Eli. All of this sounded counterintuitive.

"You go to the press," Roberta said triumphantly. "I can help you craft a statement, and you call the son of a bitch and his father out on everything. Lay it out there before they see it coming and plead with the powers that be to intervene and investigate what you're claiming. If Eli and Clive Strauss are coming to silence you, then you have to get a jump on them."

"No way," Trixie said, backing up in her chair as far as she could. "I am not going to call them out. Eli will lose his mind. Clive will ramp up whatever he was about to do and come at me with all he's got."

"They're likely going to do that anyway. The only difference is once they pick you up and take you back to Nevada, whatever voice you had is gone. This is your best shot at telling your side of the story before it can be distorted and slandered," Roberta explained.

"Can't you draft up some kind of contract or agreement?" Trixie pleaded. "You can tell them I'll never say anything about the abuse and the cover-ups, and all I want in return is to be left alone."

"I'm sure his next girlfriend would appreciate that," Roberta replied and stared, stone-faced. "You have a responsibility to tell the truth. If you're saying we have a U.S. Senator who's pulling strings to protect his son, that's conspiracy, abuse of power, and a litany of other things. This could be huge."

"With all due respect," Jamie cut in, hardly meaning those words at all, "she's not looking for this to be huge. She's looking for this to go away so she can live her life. To me it sounds like you just want a big high-profile case."

"Jamie," Travis scolded, but Roberta waved him off.

"I grew up with an alcoholic father." Roberta finally looked up from her computer as she spoke. "He beat us more than he hugged us, and my psychiatrist is pretty sure that's why I am a workaholic and relentless in my pursuit of justice. I don't make friends; I make powerful arguments. I feel for your plight, Trixie, but at the end of the day Jamie is right. I want to toss a powerful asshole in jail because that's my version of a drug. It's what I live for. It might make me cold and sound indifferent, but it also makes me the person you want in your corner. I say you go to the press in the morning, and you hit them with everything you've got. There are wolves coming for you, so either be a sheep or a bear, only one of those stands a chance of surviving. I am going to do the hard work tonight and gather up every single piece of evidence I can."

Roberta closed her laptop and tucked it into the designer bag before slinging it over her shoulder. She didn't say another word. Like a boss she just nodded and showed herself to the door.

"That lady is kind of scary," Travis admitted as he peeked out the window to ensure she was gone.

Jamie put his arm around Trixie who looked like her wobbling legs might give way. "Scary is a good thing. We could use more of it on our side."

"What do you think you're going to do?" Autumn asked, handing Trixie a tissue for the tears that were threatening to spill over.

"It gives me a lot to think about," Trixie said, pursing her lips. Jamie had the urge to push her harder. She was lost at sea and a ship had finally thrown her a line. All she had to do was reach out and take it. Why was she hesitating?

CHAPTER FOURTEEN

"Are you asleep?" Jamie heard Trixie whisper from the other couch in the living room. He was tempted to lie quietly and pretend he was. He loved hearing her voice, but he knew he might not like what she had to say.

"I'm up," he finally replied, rolling over so he was facing her on the adjacent couch.

"I know Travis and everyone else is happy we're here. But I think I made the wrong decision. Maisie and I are leaving." He could see she'd already quietly packed some of their things.

"You're scared, Trix. That's to be expected, but we need to stay the course. You're doing the right thing, and people are here to help you." He sat up and stretched the ache out of his back. He knew even as he spoke it wouldn't deter her.

"I think you should stay, Jamie. As much as I want you with us, I can see this is where you belong. Even if you don't want to say it out loud, this is your family."

"There's no reason you don't belong here too." Jamie

crossed the living room and sat beside her. "They're good people."

"I know," Trixie said, waving off the idea that she was implying otherwise. "They're such good people they don't deserve the fight I'm going to bring to their doorstep. We'll be fine. I really believe Maisie and I can make a fresh start somewhere. I don't want you to worry about us."

Jamie laughed, which probably seemed out of place considering how serious this conversation was, but he couldn't help it. "Travis always tells me you don't get to decide who worries about you. The only thing you can control is trying to give them fewer reasons to. I never thought I'd be saying that to anyone else."

"I can't stay, Jamie." Trixie stood and slid her feet into her shoes. "There's nothing you can say."

"Oh, but there is." Jamie sighed. "Come outside with me." He took her by the hand and led her out to Autumn's front step. "Travis has his reasons for wanting me to do this right. He believes I can help you, but not on my own. That's because I've been in this position before." Jamie took a seat on the top step and gestured for her to do the same. She looked at her watch as though he was eating into the hours of her head start. "The money I had you put in the bank for me was for my mother's care at a mental institution."

"And you didn't want anyone to know you were a good enough guy to try to take care of your mother? Why hide that?" She scrutinized him as though he might only be trying to stall her.

"I don't care who else knows as long as she doesn't. I'm not sure how frequently she's lucid, but I hate her, and she doesn't deserve to know I'm paying for her care." Jamie drew in a deep breath, understanding what he said wouldn't end the conversation, it would only spur more questions. "She's got all sorts of mental problems," he continued. "Hallucinations, voices, and manic episodes. I think it got worse when I was about eight or nine. I got really good at making her better though. I knew when she needed to be alone, when she needed more meds, and when she'd be all right for a little while. There were certain songs on the radio that would calm her and others that would enrage her. I figured it all out, and she got better."

"That's good, but an awful big burden for a little kid," Trixie said empathetically. But he knew he'd only pulled back one layer of his history. The deeper he'd go the less she'd be able to relate.

"She got so much better she started dating this guy. I was about ten by then, and we didn't get along much. Mostly because I knew he had no idea she was sick. He didn't know how much medication it took for her to be normal. Or at least to pretend to be." He unlaced his boot, tightened it, and tied it back up, trying to keep his hands busy as he bore his soul. "She got pregnant. It was twins, and she had to come off most of her medication. The guy stuck around maybe two weeks, and then he bolted. It was just us again, but now we were in way over our heads."

"Twins," Trixie said, shaking her head. "That must have been pretty scary for you."

"It was at first, but I figured things out. I got the house ready for the babies. I read a ton of books, and I tried to keep my mom as calm as possible. We only had some welfare checks and healthcare subsidies, but we made it work. I didn't need much. The babies came, and they were healthy. We got through it. I remember a social worker coming to the house once or twice, wondering if my mother was fit to raise the babies. Once I figured out they'd be taken away if my mom wasn't well, I started assuring them everything was taken care of all the time. My entire goal for the next few years was to make sure no one ever came and split my family up. Through the good days and the bad days I made sure we looked safe and normal enough to not raise any flags."

"How in the world did you keep that up for so long? I know grown people who can't raise twins without a lot of help. You were a child with a sick mother doing it, that's astonishing."

"I always thought if I asked for help that would be when they'd come take us away and split us up. So I never talked to anyone. When I turned fifteen I started working a few hours on an overnight shift at a mill next to our house. I could walk there, and my sisters were old enough to sleep through the night and mostly take care of themselves. My mom took so many pills she was always out cold. But I guess I was tired or distracted or whatever and didn't realize she'd been skipping doses."

"They would have been about Maisie's age," Trixie deduced. "I can't imagine Maisie having to take care of herself."

"I know," Jamie said solemnly. "I was crazy to think that. Even crazier to think my mother could be considered managed."

"You can't put that on yourself. If you were working, going to school, and raising your sisters you couldn't be expected to keep your mother medicated properly every minute of the day." Trixie did what most people did, tried to take the burden of guilt off Jamie's shoulders. Those were wasted words. It was impossible to lift the weight off him.

"One night my mother got up and was having some kind of manic episode. After spinning out of control, she went in the kitchen and started cooking something. I still don't know what she was trying to make. But the kitchen caught on fire. Our house was tiny and old. It went up so fast. My mother stumbled out the front door and sat down on the lawn, watching the house burn to the ground like it was a fireworks show on the Fourth of July. By the time the neighbors called the fire department it was too late. My sisters were gone," Jamie choked out the words but didn't cry. He was well beyond that now. It wasn't that he had come to terms with their deaths; he'd just practiced acting like he had.

Trixie didn't speak. She just raised her hand to her mouth and closed her eyes. He knew she wasn't expecting that outcome. Maybe Jamie would say the girls were taken away, whisked off to foster care, and adopted by someone. Maybe they went on to be with family somewhere far away, but she clearly wasn't ready to hear they were dead. He still couldn't believe it himself.

"My mother was committed immediately, and I was put into foster care. Trust me, no one was looking to adopt a sixteen-year-old kid who was so angry he couldn't be controlled. I ended up in a halfway house until Travis found me. For the last five years all I've done is hate myself and made anyone who's tried to love me miserable. I took too many pills, drank too much, drove too fast, and stole things just for the fun of it. I got a letter a few months ago that a private company had purchased my mother's treatment facility, and if a resident wanted to stay they'd need to pay out of pocket now.

"That's why Travis was surprised you were here asking for help?" Trixie asked, sucking in a deep breath as she tried to process everything.

"Right. He's bailed me out of hundreds of situations, but not because I ever asked for help. Someone would call him, and he'd come running, and the whole time I'd act like I didn't even want him around. For me to show up here and ask him for help, it means something."

"I hear what you're saying," Trixie assured him, but her body language was not that of someone who had been swayed.

"Do you?" Jamie asked. "Because I have never talked about my sisters with anyone. I've been court ordered to therapy, I've had dozens of people try to get me to talk about it, and I never have. Even what Travis knows about it comes from what's been discussed in court."

"So that's why you're so good with Maisie?" Trixie asked as though pieces of the puzzle were still sliding into place in her mind. "What were their names?"

Jamie shook his head and closed his eyes. "No," was all he could manage.

"Okay," Trixie said quickly. "I'm sorry; it's okay."

"I needed you to know I've been where you are before. I was in a place where I thought getting help from people around me was more dangerous than doing it all on my own. But maybe if I had asked for help my sisters would be alive. They could have been adopted by some nice couple and be living the life they deserved. Maybe my mother would have been given help sooner, and I wouldn't hate her the way I do.

I know you're scared for Maisie, but I think you have a better chance at keeping her safe if you do what the lawyer is advising."

"But your mother was sick," Trixie argued. "Eli is just a monster. I know exactly how he reacts when he is provoked. And his father will not tolerate a scandal. We'd be taking away my one shot of making all this go away."

"Trix," Jamie pleaded, "this will not just go away. It's already national news."

"Maybe you're right," Trixie shrugged, leaning her head on his shoulder. "Let's go back inside. I'm exhausted."

He stood first and extended his hand, pulling her to her feet. He knew she hadn't given up the idea of leaving, but at least she wasn't going anywhere right this minute. She stayed, face to face with him, looking up into his eyes. "I'm sorry you hate yourself, Jamie. I know there's nothing I can say to change that, but it's important you know I don't hate you. Maisie doesn't either. We might actually love you. And you deserve to be loved. I see how you look at Travis. You respect him and admire how he's helped you. Well, to us, you're just as good. You've done for us what he did for you."

Jamie dropped his head to her shoulder as she pulled him into a hug. Her hand came up and ran through the hair on the back of his head. She held him like a mother might hold a child, comforting him with some whispers in his ear. "You're just as good," she murmured again. When he pulled his face back, their mouths were just inches apart.

He wasn't sure who leaned in first, who closed the gap and turned the moment from emotional to physical. It didn't matter. When their lips touched, whatever ache he was feeling melted away. They were no closer to knowing how all this would end. He was still a guy who buried his sisters and blamed himself. She was still a woman who had danger nipping at her heels. But for this brief moment, as their bodies came together, none of that mattered. There was a tiny voice in his head saying, *It's all going to work out. All I need is this, right here.*

CHAPTER FIFTEEN

Jamie spent the rest of the night dreaming about Trixie's body. They'd quietly slipped away to her car and made love, unable to keep their hands off each other after that kiss. When they snuck back into the house, his tired body needed very little time to drift off to a peaceful sleep.

He was right in the middle of a dream about the curve of her hip and her silky skin when he heard Travis's voice and felt a kick to his leg.

"Wake up," Travis said impatiently.

"What?" Jamie groaned, assuming he might be getting an earful about the impulsive little outing in the car in the middle of the night. Had they woken them up?

"She's gone," Travis said, flashing a note in Jamie's face.

Jamie shot up and took the note from his hand hastily. The only word written on the back of a picture Maisie had colored was, *sorry*. That's it. That was all she'd done in the way of an explanation or a goodbye.

"I talked to her last night. She looked ready to bolt. I told her about," he hesitated, looking over at Autumn and deciding to just spit it out. "I talked to her about my mom and my sisters. I told her everything, Travis."

The look on Travis's face changed from frustrated confusion to one of a parent who sees their child fail or fall. It was a helpless kind of sadness. "If she was set on going, you couldn't stop her." He tried to help, but Jamie was already up, pulling on a shirt and looking for his shoes.

"We were awake three hours ago," Jamie said, looking at the clock. "She couldn't have gotten very far. Let me borrow your car." His hand was out, expecting keys would be placed in his palm without hesitation.

"Jamie," Autumn said, stepping in closer, "she made her choice. Even if you find her, she won't come back. Trixie is trying to do what she thinks is best for her and her daughter."

"I don't care if she won't come back. She doesn't have to, but she does have to take me with her. I'm going wherever they go. I can't believe she left without me." He paced around the kitchen, running his hand through his hair as though it might jump-start his confused brain.

"It's because she cares about you," Travis explained. "She doesn't want you caught up in this, and maybe you should honor that choice. I know you want to help her."

"No, I *have* to help her. I made a commitment to her the day she got in my car and drove out of Vegas. She can't do this alone. He will find her."

"We can call the police, and you can make a statement about what you witnessed in Vegas," Autumn said. "I'll have Roberta come back this morning, and she can give us options."

"Stop," Jamie shouted, turning and punching the wall

behind him. His fist broke a hole in the sheetrock, tearing the wallpaper, and marking it with blood.

"Jamie," Travis roared, making a move for him but Autumn caught his arm.

"No," Autumn said in a bolder voice than Jamie ever heard her use before. "It's just a wall. If I thought I could do that and not break my hand I'd have punched it a hundred times before. Let him be."

"He can't go after her," Travis argued. "I'm not going to lose him."

"You'll lose him ten times faster if you tell him he can't go," Autumn reasoned. "He's trying, Travis," she reminded him. "He's doing something for someone else. He's trying to do the right thing. Don't stand in the way of that."

"Trav," Jamie said, shaking the ache out of his hand, "I think maybe I could actually . . . I mean I know it hasn't been long, but she's different, and I think that . . ."

"Oh," Travis said, his eyes going wide, "you love her."

All Jamie could do was rest his back against the wall he just punched and nod his head yes. He slid down the wall until he was sitting.

Autumn grabbed her car keys and tossed them to Travis. "It's Friday, Travis already took the day off, and we can go look for her all weekend. We can do this together."

The men looked at each other as though they weren't sure that plan would work. Would Jamie move faster on his own? Would Travis continuously try to talk him out of looking for Trixie when things got hard?

The wheels in Travis's head were spinning in overdrive. "Someone should be here to deal with the marshals and to tell Trixie's side of the story. The truth needs to come out whether Trixie is the one to tell it or not. There are people in Vegas who know the kind of man Eli really is. You saw him yourself, Jamie. There is enough there to still do something about this legally."

"I can handle that," Autumn offered. "I'll work with the lawyer. I'll stall the marshals. I can do it."

"What if they get demanding?" Travis asked, looking skeptical. "We don't know how far they plan to go to get answers and find Trixie."

"Let them try," Autumn said, making her face look tough. "I'm a recent widow of one of the best lawyers in this town. Charlie had a lot of friends, and all of them would do anything to help me. I'll start calling in favors. When Trixie isn't at the precinct this morning, the marshal will be furious. Chances are they'll come here since that's the last place she was seen. I'll make sure I'm prepared for them."

"Thanks," Jamie said, taking Travis's hand and using it to lift himself back on his feet. "I'll take whatever head start I can get."

"We have no clue which way she went," Travis reiterated. "She could have headed in any direction."

"I will find her," Jamie said emphatically. "I know her. I'll be able to find her."

"How much do you think Chuck will cover for us?" Autumn asked, pacing around the room. "Because at this point they don't know what car she's driving. They don't know when she left. Chuck might be obligated to give the marshals as much info as he has."

"He's with us," Travis said, without skipping a beat. "I've known him since kindergarten. He's a tough ass about some stuff, but he's seen a lot of things in his career. He doesn't screw around when it comes to domestic abuse. He'll cover the best he can."

"So go," Autumn said, reaching in the pantry and grabbing a couple granola bars and some bottled water for them to take. "Go find her."

CHAPTER SIXTEEN

"I'm not sure that tone is appropriate," Roberta said with a smug chuckle. Autumn had heard endless stories from Charlie about Roberta's courtroom skills as a lawyer. He often called her the scariest person he'd ever met, but he'd always add he meant it in a good way. "You're speaking to the widow of my dear friend."

Marshal Joe Contenelli drove his teeth together so fiercely it made an audible grinding sound. This was clearly not going at all how he'd expected. The room was filled with five lawyers. All were standing behind Roberta as though they were ready for combat. "I can assure you my tone matches the urgency of this situation," Contenelli defended, but Roberta chuckled again.

"Here is what I see so far," Roberta said, stepping in closer to him and folding her arms arrogantly across her chest. "You're here talking to a friend of mine about a house guest of hers who decided to leave. Autumn doesn't know where that house guest was headed so this interrogation is unnecessary. Autumn didn't witness a crime and isn't privy to any criminal activity. So if you want to keep throwing around words like *obstructing justice* you might want to think again. You're not dealing with some junior varsity team here."

"I'll be frank, Mrs. Silverstone," Contenelli said through a clenched jaw, but she cut in again.

"It's Miss. I never married. I find men in general to be useless piles of masculine shit. But please continue." She smiled wide and waved as though she was giving the floor back to him.

"Well, Miss Silverstone, you don't know what you're dealing with here. This issue is far bigger than you or your little team. I have orders to find this girl. I won't stop until I do, and if I think for a second Autumn knows more than she's saying, I will find out. You don't make the rules here." He straightened his shoulders as though the extra inch might intimidate Roberta or the other lawyers behind her.

"You are right about that. I don't make the rules. The constitution has that covered, and no senator out in Nevada is going to find a way around that while I'm alive. It ends now." She reached into her bag and pulled out a stack of papers.

"I would not start throwing out any allegations, Miss. Silverstone. Maybe you know your way around a messy divorce or a misdemeanor case, but we're talking about the big leagues here."

"And this vagina of mine just makes me completely unequipped to take on such a formidable man like Strauss and his son, right? What I should do is step out of the way, clutch my pearls, and fan myself so I don't faint. Fuck you," Roberta said with a bite in her voice that echoed against every wall in Autumn's house. She tossed a stack of papers onto the counter. "Your boss is going down, and it's going to happen fast. You might want to decide how much loyalty you intend to give him."

"Ha," Contenelli laughed. "I'd like to see that happen. You're insane."

"Right, because any woman powerful enough to challenge a man who's been trading favors and using his political clout to keep his abusive, destructive, piece of crap son out of trouble, must be insane right? Feel free to skim through these papers I gathered up last night. In here you will find every hospital record of Trixie over the last three years."

"How did you get those?" Contenelli asked, knitting his brows skeptically. For the first time his swagger faded.

"Surprised, I can see," Roberta grinned. "You thought they'd all been *accidently* destroyed right? That's what Strauss ordered the hospital to do after he provided extra funding to their research facility. Well there were some sympathetic nurses who made copies and held on to them. They were happy to fax them over to me late last night. They remember Trixie clearly and would be pleased to testify not only that they treated her injuries again and again, but they were instructed to destroy the reports."

"There's no way to tie that to Senator Strauss. And maybe the girl is just clumsy. If that's all you've got—" He waived her off but she plowed through his words with her own.

"Oh, there is so much more. I have multiple security personnel who worked at the casino with Trixie who are willing to testify seeing the abuse firsthand. They will go on record and name names of police officers that arrived on scene and proceeded to cover-up the abuse. Their jobs were threatened, and don't bother saying that can't be tied back to the senator because you know as well as I do when these cops start getting identified and brought in on charges, at least one of them will turn your guy in."

Autumn watched, her heart thudding against the walls of her chest as this unfolded in front of her. Roberta was everything Charlie had ever described, and watching her was like watching a heavyweight champ pummel a featherweight.

"You don't want to do this, trust me. You don't know who you're messing with." The marshal fidgeted with his tie that seemed to be strangling him now.

"I've gone up against plenty in the past, and I've figured out how to make it work. You have to get enough people ready to talk all at once, so men like you can't silence them all. Even if you intimidate or discredit one, there will be two more behind them to speak up. I've got a laundry list of people ready to make a statement on the record about conspiracy, bribery, threats, misconduct, and so many more things that will drag Strauss and his kid through mud so deep they'll never wash clean."

Contenelli bit his lip as he looked at the papers Roberta had put in front of him. His blood was boiling, and the vein in his forehead was pulsing. "So what do you want?"

"I just told you," Roberta said in a steely tone.

"No, I mean what makes all this go away? You want him to back off the girl? Strauss doesn't even care about her. If she shuts her mouth about the abuse, he'll let her go. His kid's a crackpot though, so getting him to back off might be harder, but I'll get him in line." Contenelli shook his head like he couldn't believe what was happening.

"You misunderstand me," Roberta said with a wry smile. "I'm not looking for any kind of terms to make all this go away. It's not going away. He can stop chasing the girl because she doesn't matter anymore. She won't be the linchpin that brings him down. I will be. If he wants to come after someone, he can find me right here in Greenwich. I'll give him my home address. He can stop coming for Trixie, because I'm coming for him."

"You are a crazy bitch," Contenelli huffed out as he ran his hands over his shaved head in exasperation. "He will come at you with everything he's got. Why do you even care about this stupid girl and her kid? What are they to you?"

"Nothing," Roberta admitted. "I'd like to say I'm doing this because I've got a soft spot for a couple of innocent people who have been literally and figuratively beaten down by a man and his monster of a son. But that's not why I'm doing this. You see, there is this face a man makes when you take away the power he's been abusing. This crashing down body language when they realize the game is over, and they've lost. It's my favorite thing in the world. I crave it, and you just gave me a great fix of it. Now I want to be there when Strauss realizes what you already have. It's over."

Contenelli's face was blood red as he sputtered for words that wouldn't come. He slammed one hand down on the counter and rested the other on the leather that held his holstered weapon.

Autumn felt her heart skip a beat. Would a desperate man really shoot a roomful of people to stop what he thought would be his own destruction? He was a marshal, he had connections; could he really kill them all and get away with it?

"I did lie about one thing," Roberta admitted, her eyes

focused on his gun, still at his hip. "We aren't all lawyers. Dillon over there is my nephew. He's a Navy Seal."

"Good for him," Contenelli grunted as though it wouldn't stop him if he wanted to take down everyone in this room.

"He's a communications specialist. He hooked up this great set of microphones and cameras in here. Everything has been live streaming to a website. You know how the Internet works, right?" She pointed to a few of the tiny cameras. "Say cheese."

He didn't say another word as he backed out of the house and slammed the front door behind him.

No one spoke until the screech of his tires gripping the asphalt had faded and the rumble of his car engine couldn't be heard anymore.

"Now the real work begins," Roberta said, pulling her cell phone out. "This case would be stronger with Trixie's testimony. Have you heard anything from them?"

"Not yet," Autumn said, looking down at her blank phone screen. "Do you think they will leave Trixie alone now? You said she didn't really matter to them anymore."

"That was a bluff," Roberta admitted as she clicked away on her phone. "Strauss will want her more than ever. They'll want her to discount every ounce of testimony we build against him. Even if I have a long list of witnesses ready to tell the truth, a statement from Trixie that doesn't support what the witnesses are saying can hurt. I'm guessing they'll find her and do whatever it takes to have her on their side."

"But I thought you were trying to help her?" Autumn asked, feeling like maybe Roberta hadn't played the right card.

"Trust me, I am. That man was ready to do anything to

silence her. In their opinion she was the only liability they had. If she spoke up they were at risk. Now they know they're in trouble, and she's more important to them alive than dead. This probably saved her life, but if they do get their hands on her they'll use any tactic possible to get her to publically deny all the things people are willing to say they witnessed. If she does, this will be more of an uphill battle."

"What could they do to get her to come over to their side and publically support them?" Autumn couldn't imagine how that could be accomplished. Trixie hated them. She was scared of them so would she really defend the Strauss family after all she'd been through?

"My guess is they'll use her daughter as a bargaining chip. It's the only thing Trixie cares about more than her own life. If Maisie were in some kind of danger, Trixie would do anything. I'm sure they know that."

"So what do we do?" Autumn asked, nervously biting at her fingernail.

"We find her first. Dillon and his military buddies are using their skills to try to digitally track her. Even if she's not using credit cards and she dumped her prepaid cell phone, they still have ways. The problem is Senator Strauss will have the same type of favors he can call in. If we can find her, so can they. It'll just be a matter of who gets to her first." Roberta turned her back for a second and spoke a few cryptic words into her phone before hanging it up. "In the meantime my team is getting every single statement, phone record, and documentation of bribe payoffs they can. They'll build the case against Strauss and Eli."

"Roberta," Autumn said, her shoulders sinking a bit, "I'm so grateful for the help you're giving. I know you probably didn't expect a call from me and certainly not something like this."

"I truly loved Charlie," Roberta admitted, though it looked tough for her to show that level of emotion. "When other men treated me like some kind of crazy bitch he always saw me as a passionate and fierce lawyer, who deserved as much as the men in our firm. I would do anything for him, and that includes making sure you never have to go it alone with anything where I could help."

"Thank you," Autumn choked out, remembering how many lives her husband had touched and how his legacy was still keeping her safe.

"But try not to go up against any more corrupt politicians or serial domestic abusers. I was expecting you to call me about a parking ticket or something." Roberta patted Autumn's shoulder and they both chuckled. "Now let's get to work."

CHAPTER SEVENTEEN

"Thanks for the update," Travis said, hanging up his phone and tossing it into the center console. "You hear all that?" he asked Jamie, who was so anxious he felt like he'd jump out of his skin.

"Yeah," he said, sounding more frustrated than he meant. "That Roberta lady seems like she really gave it to them."

"And they're going to be texting us soon with more information about where they think Trixie may be." Travis's forced optimism kept grating at Jamie, but he reminded himself he was doing his best.

Jamie's phone rang and the screen flashed with the words *blocked number*. He clicked the button quickly and put the phone to his ear.

"Jamie," he heard Trixie say in a quiet voice.

"Trix, where the hell are you? I'm coming to you just tell me where you are." He was frantic, feeling like there was this tiny thread connecting them, and it could break at any second.

"We're fine, Jamie," Trixie said, sounding apologetic. "I

didn't mean to leave like that. I have to think of Maisie first. I know you think I can beat Eli somehow but you don't know him the way I do. You've never been with him when he's angry."

"I understand," Jamie said, speaking with such care, afraid to scare her off. "You can do whatever you want, just please let me do it with you. Don't leave me behind." His voice shook with emotion.

The line was silent. He couldn't tell if she'd hung up or not, but every second felt like an eternity. When he heard her breathe out he was relieved to know she was still there.

"We went south," she said reluctantly. "We're going through Baltimore now."

"I knew it," Jamie said, pumping his fist and switching the phone to speaker so Travis could hear it too. "We left not too long after you. Something just told me you'd head south since the last you knew Eli was heading to New Hampshire. Travis and I are going through Newark now. If you stay there I could be to you in three hours, less if Travis lets me drive."

"I . . . I," Trixie stuttered. "I don't want to stop Jamie. What if he already knows where I'm headed? I want to keep moving."

"Trixie," Travis said when Jamie couldn't muster a calm response. "There's something you need to know. The lawyer, Roberta, is going after Strauss. She's got an enormous amount of testimony and support she feels will be enough. That's even without you having to say a word. She's told the marshal that came to the house this morning that she plans to take Strauss down herself. Roberta was very clear you were not the liability to them anymore, she was."

"So you think they'll leave me alone?" Trixie asked, not

because she was hopeful but because she knew it wasn't true. She was testing them to see what they thought.

"It might mean the opposite. They might pursue you more, so they can have you there to recant any testimony or dispute any charges against them. There isn't anything more powerful than the victim in the case saying nothing actually occurred." Travis was a pro at staying calm when the world around him seemed to be falling down.

"There's something everyone is forgetting here. Eli and his father might have wanted the same thing at one point, but now they are coming from two very different places. Eli wanted me back in his grip, and his father wanted me back under control and quiet. Now his father will have bigger problems than me. Eli, however, still wants the same thing. He hates his father. He doesn't care if he burns in hell for all he's done. He's always just wanted one thing—me."

"Find somewhere to stay, and we'll be there as fast as we can," Jamie pleaded. "He has no idea what car you're driving. He doesn't know what phone you're using or what direction you went. We didn't really have any leads on you until you called. They won't either. Just give us a few hours."

"Is that Jamie?" Maisie's sleepy voice came across the line, and his head dropped down, like it was as heavy as his sad heart. He could feel Travis's eyes on him, as though he was looking at a new man. One with feelings, one who cared again about someone other than himself.

"Wait there," Jamie said. "Go somewhere with a big crowd and wait. We'll be there, and we'll work all this out. Roberta has an enormous amount of support. With it comes protection for you and Maisie."

"Can I talk to him?" Maisie asked relentlessly in the background.

"Put me on speaker," Jamie asked, clearing his anxious throat. "Hey kid," he said, trying to sound upbeat.

"Are you coming?" she asked hopefully.

Jamie didn't answer. Trixie hadn't agreed to anything yet. As much as he wished to interject what he wanted to happen, he wouldn't take that power from her. She'd been stripped of enough things over the years.

"Yes, honey," Trixie said in a forced bubbly tone. "He's coming to see us in a few hours."

Maisie squealed and clapped her hands. "I knew it," she announced proudly. "I knew he would come, Mommy.

"Always," Jamie said, without giving enough thought to how profound his statement was. "I'll always show up for you, kid."

CHAPTER EIGHTEEN

When Autumn's home phone rang, all the lawyers checked their cells and quickly realized it wasn't them. She raced over to the small table where the phone was and picked it up in a hurry.

"Put her on the phone," a gravelly angry voice demanded.

"Who?" Autumn asked, worried. Her stomach had been in knots for days, and the unfamiliar voice on the other end of the line sent the hair on the back her neck shooting to attention.

"That bitch lawyer," he demanded.

"Oh," Autumn replied, looking over at Roberta, feeling a little bad she instantly knew who the man was talking about. "It's a man asking for you, Roberta," Autumn explained, handing over the phone. Dillon stood quickly and plugged a device into the side of the cordless phone. It brought the man's voice over a speaker on the table.

"This is Roberta Silverstone," she said confidently as she stood with her back arrow straight.

"Who the hell do you think you are?" the man growled.

"That's a great question," Roberta said as though she was contemplating it. "Are you talking physiologically or spiritually?"

"Cut the bullshit," he yelled. "You want to play ball with the big boys then the least you can do is take this seriously. This is dead serious shit you are dealing with."

"Oh me, oh my," Roberta said, pretending to sound like a southern belle. "What have I gotten myself into? Wait, that's right. I could give a shit about you and your tough guy bureaucratic attitude. I'm assuming your man passed along my message to you. Everything I said still stands."

"I sit on the United States Defense Fund commission. I deal with the President on a regular basis. Do you know how many people on this planet want me exactly where I am? They need me, and they'll be damned if some bitch in Connecticut thinks she can take me down. You're not going up against me, you're going up against every person I have an agreement with."

"And Mr. Strauss, by agreement you mean backdoor deals to earmark money and decisions in order to gain favors?" Roberta didn't look rattled at all. If anything she looked like her body was coursing with adrenaline.

"I don't give warnings," Strauss grumbled. "I'm making an exception in this case. I can get you a one-way ticket to Guantanamo Bay."

Roberta let out a snicker and Autumn wondered if she was minimizing a very serious threat. But before she could even give the lawyer a look, Roberta was speaking again.

"Could we speed this up a bit Strauss? I have witnesses I'm looking to get on record in the next couple of minutes. We've already heard the threats; can we move on to the

THE RUNAWAY STORM

bribes?" She leaned her hands down onto the table to get closer to the speaker. "That's how this works, right?"

The line was silent for a long moment before Strauss spoke. "How much would it take?" he ground out.

"There's no amount of money," Roberta laughed. "I just figured we better cover all our bases before we moved on. Now we have that out of the way. I've spoken with your son's ex-girlfriends, high school classmates, and co-workers. There is a parade of people ready to talk because they know they aren't alone in this anymore. Call your damage control department. Start getting your ducks in a row. There's nowhere to go from here, Strauss."

"No matter what happens, you will pay," Strauss threatened. "I don't care if it's the last thing I do."

"Great talking with you, Senator." Roberta smiled as she disconnected the call. Rather than looking at all concerned she went straight into ordering people around. "Thomas, I want an update from Carla in the office within the next five minutes. This should all be coming together. I want to be standing in front of every news camera in the state tomorrow morning. The quicker we move the better."

Autumn's phone chirped and a long text message flashed across the screen. "Roberta, good news," she explained as she interrupted her directions to all the other lawyers around the table. "Jamie and Travis know where Trixie is. They're heading to her now."

Roberta nodded her head but grabbed her laptop and started tapping frantically as she drafted out an email.

"Isn't that great news?" Autumn asked, trying to get a read on what exactly was supposed to happen next. She wanted to give Travis an update, but she wasn't sure what she'd say.

"Frankly Autumn," Roberta said, finally looking up at her, "I hope the girl and her daughter are all right, but they aren't my concern anymore. I offered her a shot to strike first, and she chose to be selfish and leave. We'd have a much better chance if she were up in front of those cameras tomorrow rather than me. She'd be able to get the public on her side and put an actual face to the crimes of the Strauss family."

"She was afraid," Autumn defended. "You're holding onto a stack of papers and statements from people who back up her reasons for being scared. Can you blame her for leaving?"

"Yes," Roberta said curtly as she turned back to her computer. "I'm not likely to come out of this unscathed in one way or another, but I don't plan to back down. I will see this through to the end—or as far as I can."

"What can he really do to you?" Autumn asked, genuinely curious what a man like Clive Strauss was capable of doing to someone who might threaten his way of life.

"It doesn't matter," Roberta answered, waving off the idea. "I've got the support of every partner in my firm, as well as quite a few favors I've called in. Even if Strauss finds a way to take me down, one way or another this will move forward. Too many people are behind it now to stop."

"But you think it would be more effective with Trixie here in front of the cameras?" Autumn asked, moving into Roberta's line of sight so she couldn't be completely ignored.

"No doubt," Roberta said, closing her computer and tucking it into her bag. "Trixie is what matters here. She's the most recent victim, and the one who is still in imminent danger. A man like Strauss will be tried by the court of public opinion well before he ever sees the inside of an actual courtroom. Trixie and her daughter make the most compelling case for the public to connect to."

"I'll call Travis, and maybe he can convince her to come back." The rest of the lawyers were packing up their bags, taking their cue from Roberta.

"Good," Roberta smiled, but Autumn could tell she'd already written it off as a lost cause. A woman like that had no time to wait around for someone to become courageous or have a pang of conscience.

Within a few minutes everyone had left Autumn's house and taken all their stacks of papers and laptops with them. The only evidence that showed they'd been there were a few empty coffee mugs. She gathered them up and took them to the sink, feeling utterly useless. Travis and Jamie were off rescuing Trixie and Maisie. Roberta and her team were getting ready to take on some of the most powerful people in the country. All Autumn could do was load the dishwasher.

CHAPTER NINETEEN

Trixie pulled into the gas station she'd agreed to meet Jamie at and parked next to one of the pumps. She figured no matter what happened it would be good to have a full tank of gas. Jamie would be another twenty minutes according to his last text message.

"I'm going to pump some gas, honey," she explained to Maisie as she stepped out of the car and slid her prepaid credit card into the pump.

"I hate to see you looking so tired," Eli said, as he rounded the back of the car and stepped right up against her, clamping one hand down on her shoulder tightly.

"Eli," she said, squirming uncomfortably under his grip.

"Hop in the car. Give me the keys; I'll drive," Eli demanded, pressing his hands to the back window so he could get a look at who else was in the car. "I'm looking forward to it just being the three of us again."

Trixie clicked the lock button on the car and looked at her feet, trying to think quickly. It wasn't hot here like it was in Vegas. Jamie would arrive soon, and he'd see the car. He'd be able to get to Maisie. That was what mattered.

The drainage grate by her feet was deep. The cover was some kind of heavy metal and would be impossible to lift. Before Eli could reach for her wrist she did the only thing she could think to do. She dropped the keys down in the darkness of the drain and heard them splash at the bottom.

"Why the hell did you do that?" Eli demanded. "I have a car. I can just as easily take you in that, you idiot." His hand came up from her shoulder to her neck, and his finger closed tightly around it.

"I'll go with you to your car," Trixie explained. "I'll go now, and I'll go quietly, but you leave her where she is."

"I could smash the window," he hissed out, pressing the knuckles of his free hand to the glass. "I could put your head through it."

"But there's a much better chance if you start breaking glass someone is going to come over here and wonder what's going on. You and I can walk to your car right now and never look back. No one would know the difference."

"You won't leave her. I know you won't. What kind of game are you playing?" Eli spun her around and pushed her against the car, staring at her with wild eyes.

"I will leave her," she assured him, staring back just as fiercely. "I used to think the worst thing in the world would be to be without Maisie. Now I know she'll be fine no matter what. She doesn't deserve to pay for my mistakes."

"I'm a mistake?" Eli asked, punching at the glass behind her head. It made a loud thud but Trixie was relieved it hadn't cracked.

"No," she said, raising one of her hands up to his cheek.

"I think it'll be better if it's only you and me. Maybe it won't be so complicated. We can work it out."

Eli's eyes darted around, searching her face for the truth. She tried desperately to make sure she hid the fear and disgust as best she could.

"Get in my car," he said, letting go of her neck and grabbing the back of her arm instead. "You made such a mess of everything. Now I have to fix it."

"I know," she said, trying not to fight against his grip. She was no stranger to calming Eli down. She wasn't sure what he would do, but nothing seemed as important as making sure Maisie was safe. Jamie would get her.

"Why did you do this?" Eli asked, slamming the car into gear and taking off down the street with squealing tires.

"I'm sorry," she apologized quietly. "I know everything is a mess. We can come back from this. I'm really sorry."

"You should be. You took off on me. You know I don't want to hurt you. How many times have I told you that before? If you stop doing these stupid things, I'll stop getting so pissed."

Trixie nodded and folded her arms over her queasy stomach. "I know," she said again. "I was just confused. Everything is all right now."

"My father is losing his shit. He thinks you're out to get him or something. He told me to leave you alone, but you know I can't do that."

"What's he going to do?" Trixie asked, trying to change the subject from her own mistakes and their complex relationship.

"I stopped taking his calls. I don't really care what he

does. The only thing I wanted was you. I've got you now. He can go to hell."

"Where are we going?" Trixie asked, trying to take note of every street they passed as though somehow that would help her get away from him. It didn't matter. She wasn't going anywhere anytime soon. All she wanted was miles and hours between Eli and her daughter. She didn't care where they went as long as it was away.

"Somewhere right around here where we can be alone," he said, his angry scowl replaced by something softer but from her perspective equally as terrifying. The moment Eli came down from a rage was no more comforting. Normally it meant he'd want to make up, something he was usually ready for far sooner than she was. And now, it was something she didn't want at all.

"I'm really hungry," Trixie said, rubbing her stomach. "I haven't been feeling much like eating since we've been apart, but now that you're here I feel like I can finally relax."

He looked her over and sighed as though he was thoroughly annoyed, but Trixie knew better. She was feeding his ego the way someone might give a bottle to a frail animal.

"What do you want to eat?" he asked, looking around at the restaurants they were flying by.

"Remember that night when we first met," she smiled and ran her fingers through her newly cut hair. "We stopped at that little Mexican place and sat in the corner booth. It was just you and me. We had the whole place to ourselves."

"And the mariachi band played for us, over and over again." Eli's grip on the steering wheel loosened and his speed dropped closer to the posted speed limit. Those were always good indications he was relaxing.

She laughed at the memory. Not every minute with Eli was torture. They'd had their share of joy over the years. People never understood that part of it. Some days were as normal as anyone else's relationships. "Maybe we could find a place like that. I don't have my phone," Trixie said, patting her pockets to show him it was true. "I can't look anything up."

"Here," he said, handing over his phone. "Try to find something."

She looked down at the screen and considered what she could do to try to help herself. Send a text? Call 911? None of that made sense. A quick escape didn't mean long-term freedom. She needed a more permanent solution to getting out from Eli's grip.

"There's a quiet looking place about fifteen miles from here," Trixie said, flashing the screen at him so he could see what she was looking at. Under any other circumstance the thought of Maisie alone in her car would paralyze Trixie with fear. But she knew Jamie would be there by now, and Maisie would have her arms wrapped around his neck.

"You never should have left," Eli said, squeezing her hand with a mix of affection and anger. He fixed his eyes on her long enough for her to have to worry he might run the car off the road.

"It was a mistake," she said, patting his arm and praying he'd focus on the road again. When he finally did she let out the breath she'd been holding. "Everything is going to be better now."

CHAPTER TWENTY

"She's not answering," Jamie said as he dialed Trixie's number again. "I don't understand. This is the gas station she told us to meet her at."

"Isn't that her car?" Travis asked, pointing over at a pump. "Maybe she's just trying to lay low." He pulled the car up next to hers, and Jamie hopped out before it was in park.

"Trix," he called out, circling the car and then cupping his hands to the glass so he could see inside. Maisie was sitting on the floor behind the driver's seat with a stuffed giraffe clutched to her chest. He pulled the handle but it was locked.

"Maisie," he said, tapping on the glass. He knew it would scare her, and he was right. He watched her close in even tighter around herself and clutch the stuffed animal until it looked like it might pop a seam. "It's me. It's Jamie, can you unlock the door?"

Maisie looked up through her messy hair and lit with relief when she saw his face. Lunging for the lock button she clicked it as fast as her little fingers would allow. When Jamie swung the door open he had to catch Maisie, her momentum sending her flying into his arms.

"What's the matter?" he asked, running his hand over her sweet smelling hair. Her arms were wrapped so tightly around his neck he was nearly choking.

"He took Mommy," she whispered as a shiver rolled up her spine. "She locked the car and dropped the keys down into the ground."

Jamie looked down, searching to make sense of what Maisie was saying. She was so little. There was a chance she wasn't remembering right.

"There," she said, pointing at the grate on the ground.

"Okay," Jamie said, the picture becoming clear. "When was he here?"

"I don't know," Maisie shrugged.

"How long have you been sitting there?" Jamie asked, gesturing toward the back seat of the car.

"I don't know," Maisie said, now crying.

Jamie felt Travis come up behind him. "Don't worry about it, Maisie," he assured her as he patted her back. He looked at Jamie with eyes that shouted, *back off*.

"We need to know everything we can so we can find her." Jamie's voice was low as he covered Maisie's ears.

"You've already done exactly what Trixie would have wanted. You found Maisie, and you'll keep her safe." Travis looked around the gas station as though some looming threat might still be right around the corner.

"I'm going after them," Jamie insisted, handing Maisie over to Travis. Her arms and legs were latched on to his body.

"Please don't let go," Maisie begged. "Please."

"Okay," Jamie said, smoothing her hair as he whispered some comforting words. "You're fine now."

"I want my mommy," she sobbed as she sunk her face into his neck. Her tears soaked his skin, and he felt like he was being pulled in two very different directions. He wanted to find Trixie, but he never wanted to let go of Maisie either.

"I'll find her," he assured her as he gave her an extra squeeze. "I promise."

CHAPTER TWENTY-ONE

Eli cut into his steak with force, and Trixie couldn't help but stare at the blood that pooled below it. She remembered quickly what it was about him that rattled her to the core: his ability to shift emotional gears the way a tractor-trailer switched regular gears as it climbed a steep hill. Everything seemed perfectly normal at the moment, but any second that steak knife could be pointed at her face as he berated her for some mistake she'd made. The ice she stood upon was still very thin.

"This is delicious," Trixie said, forcing down another bite of her pasta. It was like lead in her stomach.

"I bet you weren't eating like this with that loser, right?" Eli said through a mouthful of mashed potatoes.

"It's very good," she said, her words intentionally dodging the trap he was trying to set for her. There was no right answer when it came to talking about Jamie or running away.

"I'm sorry for coming at you at work," he apologized. Trixie was all too familiar with this phase of their routine. The honeymoon phase was always full of apologies that didn't mean anything and promises that wouldn't hold any weight. Now, as she sat there with her eyes wide open to who Eli really was, she couldn't believe she'd ever fallen for this act. It truly was a cycle and spun so fast most of the time she thought it would be impossible to get off. Now the spell was broken. There was no pretending Eli loved her. He wouldn't wake up one morning and change into the man she always hoped he would be.

"I know that you don't do any of it on purpose Eli," Trixie started, but silenced abruptly when a waitress came to refill their water glasses. When the coast was clear she continued, but he cut her off.

"I wouldn't have to be so crazy if you didn't act the way you do," he defended. "You don't need to be messing around with some guy outside the casino. Your job is in the casino. It makes me look like an idiot to have my girl parading around."

This was normally where she would argue how ridiculous it was to demand she not talk to anyone but him. This time however she knew there was no point. It wasn't as if she was going to live out the rest of her life with Eli. All she needed to do was keep him from getting upset.

But what couldn't be accounted for were triggers to his anger that had nothing to do with her. His phone chirped loudly, just as it had been doing for the last hour, but this time he finally snatched it from the table and read the messages coming across.

"He's losing his mind," he grunted out. "He keeps telling me if I'm with you, I better get my ass back to Vegas right now. I'm supposed to make sure to take you to him. Like he's a king or something."

"Why would he want me there?" Trixie asked, feeling the knot in her stomach pull even tighter.

"Something about this lawyer busting his balls. He thinks you're the only one who can get her to shut up about it." He put the phone up to his ear and listened to a voicemail. The very subtle changes in the corners of his mouth sent sirens jolting through her brain. "Get the check," he demanded.

"What's wrong?" she asked, knowing whatever voicemail his father had left had him wanting to leave the restaurant immediately.

"This isn't just some bitch lawyer giving my father a hard time. She's coming after me too. She's digging up all sorts of shit." He slammed his knife down on the table and glared at her. "He says he wants you to deny all of it. You need to make a public statement saying this lady is crazy."

"I'm sure it'll blow over," Trixie said, waving at the waitress to bring them their check. "But I'll do whatever you want. I can make a statement."

"What did you already tell this lady?" Eli asked, narrowing his eyes and scrutinizing her reaction.

"Nothing," she insisted. "The people I was with, they were worried about your dad. He's a very powerful man. I didn't give any specific details about anything. I left. When you found me I was alone, right?" She was trying to convince him, but there was always a moment with Eli where you could tell it was too late. Once his mind had been set on something it didn't matter. Rage made him deaf and blind to logic.

"You must have said something," he ground out as he signed the check and pushed his chair back, thudding against the wall behind him. "They've got all sorts of stuff. Medical records from times you went to the hospital. Statements from guys you worked with that think they can come up against me."

He grabbed her wrist and pulled her through the door. "I didn't tell her about any of that. The woman, the lawyer, Roberta, she wouldn't listen to me. I tried to tell her she needed to back off of you. She's relentless."

"Now you can find a way to fix all of this." He opened up the back door of his car and threw her in. They weren't a couple anymore, riding around the front seat of the car. She was now a captive. He reached into the pocket behind the front seat and grabbed a roll of duct tape. Trixie didn't even bother fighting. Clamping her wrists together she let him wrap a few loops of tape around. Her ankles were next, and as claustrophobic as it made her feel to be tied up, she knew this was still not the time to fight him. "My father is on his way out here now. He'll expect you to make all of this right."

"I will," she said, blinking back her tears. "I'll do whatever you want, Eli."

Eli got into the front seat and peeled out of the parking lot, slamming Trixie into the back seat. "How many times have I told you that you need to keep your mouth shut? I don't say that for my own good, it's for yours too. I've given you everything. Who was there for you when you and your kid had nothing? I took her in like she was my own. You've never had to worry about anything."

The answer at the tip of her tongue was that she was worried all the time. He may have put a roof over her head, but she was also constantly afraid it could come crashing down on her any minute. The security he provided had many strings attached. And those strings had nearly strangled her to death.

"Just tell me what to do," Trixie said, trying to adjust her body as comfortably as possible against the back of the seat.

"We're not going to come back from this, Trix," Eli said, shaking his head manically. "This is done. Do you really think there will be a happily ever after? You screwed it up. You ruined it."

Her stomach sunk like an anchor, and the tears she'd been holding back began to fall. That was the one thing she hoped he wouldn't say. Eli never broke things off, no matter how bad it got. He'd always tell her he was sorry and they could work it out. If he was saying it was over, that things had been broken beyond repair, then she didn't stand a chance. He'd have no purpose for her even if his father did. But Maisie was with Jamie by now. He'd know exactly how to cheer her up and make her feel safe. Right now they'd be doing something silly, and even though he'd be worried sick about her, Jamie would put Maisie's needs first. And that's why she knew she loved him.

CHAPTER TWENTY-TWO

"We need to call the police," Travis said, unable to stay quiet any longer. He'd wanted Jamie to get to that conclusion on his own.

"We need to find Trixie," Jamie replied as he clicked Maisie into her car seat. She already had the headphones on and was clicking through different games she could play on his tablet. She had been so worried when they'd first arrived, but some assurance from Jamie that her mother was just fine seemed to work. And when all else failed for a four-year-old, distraction was still the best medicine.

"Who knows where he's headed with her right now? We call the police. Let them pull the surveillance tape and see she's been taken against her will. They'll know exactly what to do." Travis clipped his seat belt and implored Jamie to do the right thing.

"She wouldn't want that," Jamie explained. "Maisie would be taken away immediately. She'd want her to stay here with me."

"You can't just keep the little girl like she's a stray puppy.

There is a process for these things, and you know that. The police will find Trixie, and Maisie will be back with her. But none of that can happen if you don't call."

"He couldn't have gotten very far. We can have them pull up the tape and tell us what direction he headed with her. We can track them down." Jamie turned to Travis.

"And then what? We just ask Maisie to sit around while you pummel the guy and try to save her mother. You have no idea what this guy is capable of, and you want her to have a front row seat to that? There is one right way to handle this. Grow up and accept that."

"Take her back to Autumn's house," Jamie said, hopping out of the front seat and grabbing a screwdriver out of the trunk. He opened the door of Trixie's car. Kneeling by the door, he pulled back the panel under the steering wheel and hotwired the ignition, a little trick learned from a buddy in his halfway house. When the engine roared to life he hopped in and sped off, not even glancing up at the rearview mirror. He didn't need to. Travis would get Maisie to safety. There was no way he'd watch her be marched off by some agent from Child Services.

He searched the Internet for the phone number of the gas station and keyed it in. "What did the car look like?" Jamie asked. It had only taken rambling off Chuck's badge number and credentials to get the clerk jumping through hoops for him. It wasn't the first time Jamie had used it to get information out of someone.

"It's a blue SUV with plate number 22KD49. It pulled out of our lot and went left. That leads right toward the interstate, the southbound ramp. What else can I do for you, officer?"

"I appreciate the help," Jamie said curtly as he hung up the phone and looked for the next phone number he needed. "Chuck," Jamie said, knowing this was a long shot. "I need you to get me the number of that marshal who came by the house. He's in the senator's pocket, right? He'll know where Eli took Trixie."

"Slow down, kid. Travis just called and filled me in," Chuck said in a raspy whisper. "I'm still at the precinct getting torn a new one for letting Trixie run off. No one gives a shit that this guy is crazy or abusive. We're getting calls from higher-ups left and right telling us to back off of it."

"So just give me the number of that marshal, and I'll get it out of him." Jamie sped down the freeway, dodging cars like he was in a video game.

"He's not going to tell you anything. He's another wacko. I'm not sure what the play here is, Jamie. They're going to want Trixie on their side, downplaying any kind of accusations. At least Maisie is safe."

"That's the senator's strategy. But I've known plenty of guys like Eli. He's not thinking big picture or saving his ass. The only thing he wants is Trixie, and when that unravels he's going to be unpredictable. She's not safe with him. The cops aren't going to do anything, and whatever Roberta is planning won't help in time. I need to find her, and the marshal is the only lead I have. Give me his phone number. That's all I'm asking."

The line was silent long enough for Jamie to have to pull the phone away from his ear and check to make sure they hadn't been disconnected. "I'll text it to you," Chuck finally acquiesced. "Just be careful. I wish I had a better answer for you, but the stonewalling going on right now is outrageous.

Hopefully Roberta can get something together and take these guys down."

"I hope so too, but I'm not waiting around to find out."

When Jamie got the text message he immediately dialed the number. He knew damn well just driving south and hoping to stumble upon Trixie and Eli wasn't very probable. He needed something concrete, and this marshal was his best bet.

"What?" the man grumbled, sounding thoroughly annoyed.

"I need you to tell me where Eli has taken Trixie," Jamie demanded, trying unsuccessfully to sound cordial. Travis had told him how the marshal had acted at Autumn's house. He knew the guy was on the wrong side of all this, but maybe he could still be swayed with some logic.

"Go to hell," he spat back with an angry laugh. "You're the boyfriend, right? You should have convinced her to come back to Vegas with me. You might not agree with my methods, but I'm a hell of a lot better than that dirtbag who has her right now."

"Obviously," Jamie ground out. "That's why I'm calling you. Shit's about to go down. You can see that, right? Your boss, the senator, he's not getting out of this, but you still can. That is unless Trixie doesn't make it. If Eli kills her, you'll spend the rest of your life in jail. Every single thing you've done on their behalf will be dredged up, and you might even end up being the scapegoat if the senator plays his cards right."

"I'm going to get the girl now," the marshal admitted. "I've got a location on Eli, and I'm going to pick her up. Those are my orders, so that's what I'm doing."

"And Eli's fine with that?" Jamie asked skeptically.

"No, he isn't responding to calls or messages. He's gone radio silence. But when you have a loose cannon you make sure you can track them at all times. I know where he is, and I'm going to him. Whether he likes it or not, I'm picking up the girl. The senator wants to talk with her. Just talk."

"He wants her to pretend none of this ever happened. I'm sure he expects her to call off the dogs. But you know as well as I do things are too far along. It won't matter what Trixie does or says. Roberta is going to make this public. She's going to keep pushing until your boss goes down."

"Don't call him that," he barked. "He's not my boss. I don't work for him."

"You just do all his dirty work?" Jamie scoffed.

"He's a powerful man. The senator has some shit on me from years back. I needed that to stay quiet. I've got a wife and kids. I'm trying to serve my country. Everything I've done for the senator has been so I can keep my job. I actually do save people's lives. I keep bad guys off the street."

"Just not this one and his kid?" Jamie argued, unable to bite his tongue. "You can spin this however you want. But things are unraveling, and you know it. You give me their location and let me get there first. I'll get Trixie out of there. Just tell the senator I beat you to the punch."

"What makes you think you can handle Eli? I've been caught up with this family for the last two years. I know what they are capable of."

Jamie pushed harder on the accelerator and glanced at the clock. This was all wasted time. "You can still get out of this," Jamie explained. "Give me the information, and I'll get you in touch with Roberta. Ask for immunity. If you don't turn on them, they'll turn on you."

"I've got a family. I can't put them through that."

Jamie felt like screaming, but he kept his emotions in check until he could get the information he needed. "Their whole lives are about to change no matter what. At least this way you'll have some control over how it goes down."

"I'll text the address of their last location," he finally agreed. "I doubt you can actually give me any assurances the lawyer is going to go for that deal. But that's my best bet right now."

"I wasn't far behind them, and I think they traveled south. Get me the address, and I'll have Trixie out of there. Then if you want to meet up, I'll take you to the lawyer myself. If you're really willing to give her everything you know, I'm sure it'll work out for you."

"I just sent the text. Watch your back though. Who knows what you're walking into?"

"It's Eli who needs to watch out," Jamie corrected as he hung up the phone and directed all his attention back to driving as quickly as he could. He was only thirty minutes out from where Eli was holding Trixie. The way he was driving he could cut that down by half.

CHAPTER TWENTY-THREE

If this had been a cartoon, the laps Autumn had walked around her living room would have left a rut in the wood. The house was too quiet, and she felt utterly useless with everything that was going on. Once Roberta and her associates left, Travis went to radio silence, and Autumn started counting the minutes as though she could will the clock to move faster.

When she heard the rumble of a car engine pull into her driveway she fought the urge to hide. Instead she peeked from behind her lace curtains and felt a wash of relief when she saw Travis. But that feeling was fleeting. Jamie was not in the passenger seat, and as Travis plucked Maisie from the car seat, her stomach sank with worry. No scenario she could imagine made sense with Travis and Maisie showing up here on their own. The sun was setting behind them, and the light cast on the little girl's curly mop of hair looked like a halo.

Autumn moved toward the door and swung it open, trying not to look too desperate for answers, even though she was. Travis shot her a look before she could get a single question out. She interpreted it as, *not in front of the kid.*

She nodded her head slightly and plastered a smile on her face. "Hey again," she chirped to Maisie, but Maisie recoiled into Travis's arms. Her cheeks were flush, and her eyes glistened with tears.

"I know you're worried about your mom," Travis said as he placed her down on the couch. "But it's all going to work out. For now you can stay here with Autumn and me. We'll order some pizza and play games."

"I don't have games," Autumn said, looking at Travis sideways. When he gave her a quick smile she changed her tune. "I have other things we can do though."

"No," Maisie whined as she shook her head. Before Travis or Autumn could comfort her, a rainbow waterfall of vomit shot from her mouth. It splattered to Autumn's hardwood floors and was punctuated with a loud cry from Maisie. "Mommy," she begged as she looked down at the vomit and wondered what was happening to her body.

"It's okay," Autumn assured her as she ran toward Maisie, her sock slipping in the mess. She landed hard on her rear end. Travis came up quickly behind her, but rather than offering her a hand, he lifted Maisie up from the couch, inducing a little more vomit. This time it sprayed even farther, hitting the wall.

"What do we do?" Autumn asked in a panic. "Do we take her to the hospital?"

"No," Travis replied quickly. "She's not even supposed to be here. If we do that they'll take her into child protective services. I want to give Jamie time to find Trixie."

"You mean you're not supposed to even have her?"

Autumn asked, leaning away from him so she could watch every twitch of his body as he answered.

"Not technically. I am a licensed foster parent, but if child services got involved right now they wouldn't just leave her here with me. There would be an investigation. Maybe Trixie has family, and Maisie could be sent there. I'm temporarily not telling anyone she's here." Travis ran his hand over his unshaven cheek as though he could hardly believe what he was saying.

"That doesn't sound like you at all. You're a stickler for the rules." Autumn tried to wipe the mess off her clothes as she scrutinized Travis's expression.

"I know," he agreed. "I have been involved in plenty of cases with families who have been in and out of the child protective service system. If I was objectively being asked about a situation like this I would never suggest someone do what I'm doing. But look at her." He pointed at Maisie whose lip was quivering and eyes were wild with confusion.

"What's wrong with her?" Autumn ask, gesturing down at the vomit. "She's sick. We need to do something."

"Do you know any nurses or anything?" Travis asked, trying to keep his voice calm.

"What about Noah?" Autumn suggested, her face lighting with hope. "I've kept in touch with him over the last few months. He's doing well."

"The last time I saw him he was on the side of the road thinking about killing himself. You both lost your spouse's in the same car accident. Are you sure seeing each other is healthy? Doesn't it bring back a lot of stress? Is he even practicing medicine again?" Travis asked skeptically.

"I think seeing each other is actually a good thing. I don't think he's working at the hospital again, but he still has his license. I know that for sure. I'm going to call and ask him to come over. We need help." Autumn scurried into the kitchen and grabbed her phone.

She wasn't sure what she'd even said to him, but fifteen minutes later he was at her door with a medical bag in his hand. The mess had been all cleaned up, and a big pot had been placed next to Maisie on the couch. She was sleeping now, but her tiny hands still clutched her stomach.

"Thank you so much for coming, Noah," Travis greeted him and reached out his hand to shake.

"I'm not even sure why I'm here. Is it your father-in-law, Autumn? Is he sick?" Noah slipped out of his coat and hung it on a hook by the door.

"No, Mike is fine. He's getting treatment in Boston, and it's going well. We have a little girl here who threw up. We don't know what to do." Autumn gestured to Maisie on the couch.

"Who is she?" Noah asked, clearly reading the awkwardness in the situation.

"It's very complicated," Travis began but made no attempt to elaborate. He just nervously rung his hands and rocked back and forth on his heels.

Noah moved closer to Maisie and then nodded. "It must be, considering I saw her on the news a couple days ago. Isn't she the little girl who went missing out of Nevada with her mother?"

"They were running, not missing," Travis said in a hushed voice. "The mother's ex-boyfriend is a piece of work. He's grabbed her mom from a gas station south of here and left Maisie in the car. I brought her back here until Jamie can help sort it all out. I know as a doctor you have an obligation to report this to child services, but—" Noah waved Travis off.

"It's no problem. You and Autumn are fine people, and we can pretend I was never here. Now tell me what's going on with her."

"She's puking," Autumn announced, gesturing down at her own stained clothes. "Like projectile rainbows."

"How long has she been asleep?" Noah asked, looking down at his watch.

"Oh my gosh, were we not supposed to let her fall asleep?" Autumn asked in a panic. "That's a thing isn't it? Like you have to keep them alert, right?"

"That's for a concussion," Noah explained. "She didn't hit her head did she?"

"No," Travis answered. "She was quiet in the car, but I figured it was because she was worried. A few minutes after we got here she threw up. She said her stomach hurt. Autumn didn't have a thermometer, so we haven't checked her temperature, but she felt hot to me."

"I'll check her vitals, but it sounds like she is either having a response to stress or picked up a bug somewhere along the way." Noah moved in and lifted Maisie's small wrist to check her pulse. She stirred slightly but quickly fell back to sleep. He pressed a thermometer to her forehead and then felt her glands below her jaw line. "She does have a slight temperature, which makes me think she's fighting off a stomach bug. I don't think you have anything to worry about."

"But what do we do?" Autumn asked, feeling fearful that Noah might abandon them.

"Fluids, some children's fever reducer, rest, and watch

her temperature. I can leave you this thermometer if you need me to. If she goes over one hundred three give me a call.

"What kind of fluids? Fever reducer, like a medicine? Can she swallow a pill?" Autumn's questions shot out rapid fire, and Noah couldn't help but laugh a little.

"I'll make you a list," he assured them, but before he could even reach for a pen she was shooting down that suggestion.

"Can't you just stay?" she begged. "You're a doctor, and you know what you're supposed to do."

"I would, but I have a flight tomorrow afternoon I have to get prepared for. I have a lot of packing and planning to do."

"Can't you just delay the trip?" Autumn asked as though he were the one being unreasonable. Travis cut in sounding overly calm in her opinion.

"Where are you traveling to?"

"I'm starting with the Doctors of the World charity. I'll be flying for hours upon hours tomorrow, which is why I can't change or delay the flight. Too many connections to have to make."

"That's an amazing challenge to take on," Travis continued, obviously not feeling the lasers Autumn was shooting from her eyes.

"My wife had a vision of me, and I was lucky for that. She looked at me like I was a super hero. I want to go be the doctor," he shook his head as he corrected himself, "the man she always knew I could be."

"I bet she'd want you to take care of this little girl," Autumn challenged, and Noah chuckled again.

"If you really feel like you need reinforcements, I know the perfect person. Let me make a phone call."

Noah disappeared into the kitchen as he explained the scenario about Maisie to someone on the other end of the line. He came back looking fully triumphant. "Donna is on her way," he announced. "My mother-in-law has babysat hundreds of kids and knows her way around a stomach bug. You'll be in good hands. She'll even pick up all the supplies you need. Noah tucked his instruments into his bag and stood. "I better go. Call me if that fever spikes."

"Won't you stay to see Donna?" Autumn asked, curious where their tense relationship had left off.

"I'm going to see her in the morning before I leave. It'll be emotional enough, no need to start the goodbyes tonight." He nodded his head, slipped into his coat, and went out the door.

Less than ten minutes later Donna Ripper was cruising through the same door like a fairy godmother about to shower them with their deepest desire. "Hello dears," she sang as she handed Travis a heavy box. "How's our little patient?"

"She's been sleeping a little while now; maybe she's better." Travis peeked at Maisie who was starting to stir.

"She's got a whole lot more in her tummy to get rid of first, I'm sure. We better assemble the vomit bucket now while we have time."

"The vomit bucket?" Autumn asked squeamishly.

"Yes, there is one proper way to make a bucket for a stomach bug victim. First," she sang as she pulled some things out of the box, "you need a small deep trashcan like the ones you have in the bathroom. Line it with a plastic grocery bag, but make sure there are no holes in it. That defeats the purpose. Then you need to put five or so paper towels at the bottom of the bucket. Then another bag and so on."

"Why?" Autumn asked, watching Donna assemble this thing.

"The paper towels are so she doesn't get splashed in the face and the extra layers are because sometimes you think they are done being sick, you pull out the bag, and they are sick again." Donna propped the bucket down next to Maisie and began rubbing her back. "Do you want a cold cloth for your head?"

Maisie nodded and closed her eyes. "I want my mommy," she sniffled. Donna gathered the girl up into her arms and glanced over at Autumn.

"Do you have a rocking chair?" Donna asked as she began rhythmically and gently swaying back and forth.

"Upstairs," Autumn answered quickly. "Travis can bring it down." A few minutes later Donna was humming a quiet lullaby while rocking Maisie back to sleep.

Autumn looked over at Travis who stood against the wall nibbling nervously on his fingernails. He alternated between checking his phone and his watch. She could tell he was desperate to hear some news from Jamie.

"Noah wanted to stay," Autumn lied.

"He didn't," Donna countered. "But it's nice of you to say that. Things are actually getting better between us. Noah has this big trip planned. I'm sure he told you about it. I think it's wonderful, but it's also got me worried. I'm not sure he's ready to take on something so big. But he's dead set on being better than he was in every way possible."

"We all have to get through this in our own way," Autumn offered, but she knew it sounded hollow.

"I think she'll probably sleep for the rest of the night,"

Donna whispered as she put Maisie down gently on the couch and put the little bucket by her side.

"Thank you for coming over," Autumn said sincerely. "We were in way over our heads. We still might be." She let out a tiny nervous laugh.

"I'm only ten minutes down the road. If you need anything don't hesitate to call. Some people love chocolate, others curl up with a good book. For me, taking care of people is what gives me the warm and fuzzy feeling."

"How about some tea?" Travis asked, maybe for the sake of not wanting her to go yet. "I'm happy to boil some water."

Donna looked back at Maisie who stirred slightly then settled. "I guess one cup would be nice."

CHAPTER TWENTY-FOUR

Jamie spotted the rundown motel and cut the wheel hard to make sure he didn't pass it. His tires screeched, and he cursed himself for making a noise that might draw attention. He saw the car that matched the description of Eli's and felt his stomach flip over.

"Nice entrance," a low voice called out from behind him, and he spun quickly to see who it was. "Relax, it's me, Marshal Contenelli." The man flashed his credentials and raised his arm up to show he was not a threat.

"What the hell are you doing here? We had a deal. Let me get Trixie, and I'll take you to Roberta."

"I couldn't wait," he said, looking a little sheepish. "I called her myself. At the end of the day the only thing that really matters to me is my wife and kids. And if this is going down now then I can't hesitate. She's working with some contacts to get my family put in protective custody. She didn't exactly offer me immunity, but we'll hammer out the details later. I figured I'd come back you up."

"I don't need back up," Jamie barked as he shoved by him.

He tried to mentally prepare himself for whatever he might find in that hotel. Maybe Eli had beaten Trixie. What if she had been tortured or he forced himself on her? But he knew no matter what she had been through he would get her out safely. They'd leave that motel room together, and he'd help put her back together, no matter what.

He drew his leg up and kicked at the door, snapping the chain clear off and sending wood splintering in every direction. He had been wrong. He wasn't prepared for what he found. Not even close.

"What the hell?" Contenelli asked as he moved into the room, shoving Jamie forward slightly. It put him into motion, and he raced toward the bathroom, opening the door and finding nothing. Coming back into the tiny motel room he saw Eli again. He was sprawled across the bed, his clothes filthy, his face scratched, and his eyes rolling back into his head.

"Where is she?" Jamie shouted, moving toward the bed and grabbing Eli by his mud-covered collar. "Where is Trixie?"

"Gone," he moaned, trying to slap Jamie away, but whatever impaired him—drugs, alcohol, or both—made his arms useless.

"Gone where?" Jamie demanded as though he were desperately hoping the news wouldn't be as bad as it looked.

"I don't know," Eli gurgled. Jamie punched him across the face, the skin above his eye breaking open instantly.

"The last thing you want to be right now is useless. If I don't need you, I'm going to kill you. Tell me where she is." Jamie shook him, but it was no use. He was unconscious.

"Find his car keys," Contenelli instructed as he started rifling around the room.

"Why?" Jamie asked, knowing they didn't need his car for anything since they had their own.

"We need to check the trunk," Contenelli said somberly. "Plus we can look for evidence or receipts or something that can help us find her." His attempt at a positive spin fell on deaf ears. The only thing Jamie could picture now was Trixie stuffed into the trunk and not reaching her in time.

He dug through Eli's pocket, rolling his body over forcefully. When he found the keys he raced outside. Fiddling with the lock, he popped the trunk and couldn't decide if it being empty made him feel relieved or terrified. He didn't want her to be stuffed in there, but not knowing where she was didn't seem much better.

"There's some blood on the back seat," Contenelli reported. "It's not a lot though. She still might be fine. We just need to figure out where she is."

Jamie turned on his heel and raced back into the motel room. Grabbing a cup from the bathroom, he filled it then poured it over Eli's face. He came sputtering back to consciousness, gasping for air. But Jamie didn't give him even a second to get his bearings. Yanking him upright, Jamie slammed him against the headboard with a thud. "Where the hell is she?"

"I don't know," Eli choked out. "She never loved me. No one who loves you jumps out of a moving car to get away from you."

"She jumped out of your car?" Jamie asked, his skin prickly with fear. "Where?"

"I don't remember," Eli slurred out and closed his eyes.

"You better start remembering," Contenelli roared. He lunged toward Eli and shoved Jamie aside. Driving his thumb down into Eli's shoulder he went nose to nose with him. The pressure point was doing its job. "Tell me where she is, or I'll snap your neck," Contenelli hissed. His voice was so harsh Jamie couldn't tell if he was serious or the threat was empty.

"I was taking the exit," Eli forced out through his pain. "She opened the door and rolled out like a pumpkin into the woods."

"What the hell," Jamie said, cocking his fist back. Contenelli shoved him off.

"If you knock him out again we'll never find out where she is," he reminded Jamie and then directed his attention back to Eli. "Did you get out and see if she was all right?" He shoved his thumb down harder.

"I pulled over," he ground out through his clenched teeth. "I climbed around in the woods. I looked for her, but she was gone."

"So she must have been all right," Jamie said hopefully. "She got up and ran into the woods."

"Who knows," Eli said. "I was . . . I had already taken something."

"What?" Jamie demanded, not clear on what he meant.

"He was high already," Contenelli clarified. "He was too doped up to know for sure if she got away or not."

"I need to go find her," Jamie said, scrambling to his feet and making a move for the door.

"It's dark," Contenelli said as though he were stating something that wasn't already obvious. "I'll come with you. We have a better chance of finding her together."

"What about him?" Jamie asked, gesturing with his chin over at Eli.

"I'll tie him up and make sure he can't get out. We'll call the local PD and they can come pick him up."

"They'll just cut him loose. Some higher-up is going to see who he is and make the call to let him go. That's not good enough for me." Jamie balled his fists.

"We're wasting time," Contenelli pleaded. "You want to kill him then make it quick. Every second we waste is one more second you don't find Trixie."

"Just tie him up good," Jamie said curtly as he jogged to his car. A few minutes later Contenelli was jumping in the passenger seat, and they were speeding off toward the highway.

"It's this exit here," Contenelli said, pointing at the next off ramp. "Park over there on the grass. We'll start at the top and work our way down. If we don't find her, we'll make our way into the woods. But let's be strategic. I've got search and rescue experience. Where people go wrong is just wandering around, thinking they can stumble on someone who's missing. You have to have a plan."

Jamie ignored whatever he was saying and hopped out of the car after slamming it into park. He flipped on his cell phone's flashlight and started shouting Trixie's name.

"Slow down kid," Contenelli ordered, but Jamie kept moving and yelling. She had to be here. She had to be hiding somewhere just waiting to be found. "You're stomping all over what might be a crime scene."

"Just shut up and keep up," Jamie shouted over his shoulder as he searched the high grass. It was littered with discarded fast food containers and blown tire debris. Nothing looked like a clue to Trixie's location.

"Here," Contenelli shouted, pointing his flashlight at the ground. "There's a skid mark here and it looks fresh. This must be where Eli pulled off, so she would have rolled out before that. We should look back here."

Jamie turned back reluctantly. He didn't want to backpedal. He wanted to move forward and find Trixie as fast as he could. But Contenelli was trained in this and he wasn't.

"Look, there's a little blood here." Contenelli shined his light on the grass, and a few droplets of something crimson glistened. "She must have gone into the woods."

They both pointed their flashlights into the thick tree line and glanced at each other before sprinting forward. "Trixie," Jamie yelled at the top of his lungs. They both froze, hoping desperately to hear her reply. The night was still and the silence telling.

"She might have flagged down a car or gotten help," Contenelli said, but the slump in his shoulders told Jamie he didn't even believe his own words.

"Come on," Jamie insisted, pushing forward into the trees and bushes. The low shrubs were clawing at his pants and the high branches were whipping at his face.

"She wouldn't have made it this far in if she were hurt," Contenelli reasoned.

"You don't even know her," Jamie replied as he pushed forward. "She'd do anything to get back to her daughter." Jamie froze as he came across a small clearing. A bright white sock rimmed with duct tape caught the moonlight cutting through the trees. "Shit," was all Jamie could sputter before falling forward into the clearing and scurrying on his hands and knees toward Trixie.

"Don't move her," Contenelli yelled before Jamie could get his hands under her. "Just back up a little bit." He was on his knees by her side now, placing his fingers on her neck to check for a pulse.

She was face down, and Jamie's only thought was he should roll her over so the mud wasn't in her eyes. She wouldn't want all that mud on her face.

Autumn watched the level of Donna's tea as though it were a clock counting down to the apocalypse. Maisie hadn't thrown up again, and she seemed to be sleeping soundly, but that could change at any moment.

"How have things been going, Donna?" Autumn asked as she reached for the teakettle and offered her a refill.

"I'm working on the paperwork for my charity. It'll be in Rayanne's name. I want to give high school kids who want to travel abroad the opportunity. The summer she went to Paris was something she always looked back on fondly."

"That's a great idea. If there is anything we can do to help, just let us know," Travis said, and Autumn felt butterflies roll through her stomach at the ease in which he'd labeled them an *us*.

Travis's cell phone rang, and he silenced it quickly, afraid it might wake Maisie. "Jamie?" he asked, not recognizing the number but hopeful it was him. "Okay, okay, calm down."

Autumn couldn't hear what was being said on the other line, but Travis's body language was screaming something bad had happened. His immediate instinct to insist everything was okay meant it wasn't. He was off the phone a moment later and staring at Maisie with a look of helplessness, making Autumn feel like she might need one of those custom-made vomit buckets for herself.

CHAPTER TWENTY-FIVE

Jamie knew his body was giving out, but he kept ignoring the signals racing to his brain. Nothing was going to move him right now. Not hunger. Not pain. Not exhaustion. He was staying put.

"Jamie?" A voice sounded, the first noise he'd heard besides beeping machines in a while. "Jamie, I'm not sure if you remember me," the man said as he stepped cautiously inside the hospital room.

He looked the man up and down and had to force his brain to place the face. "You're the guy who almost killed himself on the side of the road. Noah, right?"

His eyes fell to the floor, likely shameful about his fall into the darkness after his wife's death. "I'm also a doctor," Noah added, inching his way a little farther into the room.

"Not at this hospital," Jamie said, looking him over skeptically.

"No, not at this hospital, but I heard about what happened, and I decided to come and see if I could help in any way. This can be very confusing, and if there are any decisions to be made it can be difficult to do that alone."

Jamie knew exactly what kind of decisions Noah was referring to, and it sent a wave of rage rolling over him. "I'm not a moron. I likely have a higher IQ than you. I don't need you dumbing down the medical jargon for me. There is a little thing called the Internet now."

"Then maybe I can just sit with you and whatever—" Noah fidgeted nervously and Jamie rolled his eyes.

"You're great at this," he groaned, gesturing with his chin at the empty chair in the corner of the room. Noah jumped at the offer and took a seat.

"My bedside manner has always left something to be desired, so I'm sorry if this is coming out wrong. I was actually supposed to fly out on a trip to the other side of the world today, but when I heard what happened I thought I should come here instead." Noah grabbed the chart that was hanging at the foot of the bed and began reading.

"Why?" Jamie scoffed.

"You know my wife died. I wasn't exactly at my best while she was alive. I'm on this kind of journey to be better. I think some of that will come from traveling and helping people who need it. But when I thought about it, if Rayanne were alive she'd tell me to come here. You shouldn't have to do this alone."

"Do what?" Jamie asked, daring the man to be negative or pessimistic. He didn't want that mindset in the room right now. He'd already made that clear to the doctor that had left a few moments before Noah had arrived.

"Help her heal," Noah said, reading the energy Jamie was

shooting in his direction. "It's not easy supporting someone who has been hurt so badly."

"And it was pretty bad, wasn't it?" Jamie asked, pulling his chair closer to the side of Trixie's bed and rubbing her motionless hand.

"This chart says the most pressing issue is her head injury. She has some broken bones and lacerations, but none of those seem life-threatening." Noah ran his finger over each note in the chart.

"But the head injury is?" Jamie asked, wide-eyed.

"Any head injury can be an unpredictable thing. Hers is serious. She went directly into surgery when she arrived at the hospital. She had a skull fracture and a brain bleed. The surgeon performed a craniotomy and repaired the bleed. He also installed a shunt that will keep any additional fluid from gathering." Noah turned to the next page of the chart and scanned it quickly.

"So is that all the good news?" Jamie asked, as he lifted Trixie's hand and kissed the delicate skin of her wrist.

"Like I said, traumatic brain injuries are volatile. They are in *wait and see* mode right now. They have her in a medically induced coma so her body can rest. Her team will watch for any swelling of the brain, which is extremely dangerous." Noah looked Jamie square in the eye as he explained what was happening.

"She could wake up and be fine," Jamie said with a raised eyebrow. "She could recover completely."

"She absolutely could," Noah assured her, shaking his head in agreement. "But no matter what happens she will have a long recovery ahead of her. The surgery she endured today has its own risks. There is a chance of infection. Her motor skills may be affected. I won't go into the list of possibilities. But know when a piece of your skull is removed and replaced, no matter what the circumstances, recovery can be long and arduous. Waking up is only part of the battle."

"She has a little girl," Jamie said, rubbing the back of Trixie's hand against his cheek. Her scent had been mostly snuffed out by the smells of the hospital.

"I know," Noah said with a tiny smile. "I met her last night. Travis and Autumn called me to take a look at her because she was sick."

"Sick?" Jamie asked. His already thudding heart ramped up another notch.

"She's fine," Noah assured him quickly. "It was a stomach bug or something. My mother-in-law, Donna, brought them everything they needed to take care of her. I checked, and there is nothing to worry about."

"Thanks for going over there. The kid has been through hell. She doesn't deserve this." He dropped his head and planted a few more kisses on the back of Trixie's hand.

"You might want to ease up on that," Noah said, gesturing toward Jamie and the affection he was showing.

Jamie looked down at her hand and looked for what damage he might be doing. "Why? I'm not hurting her."

"No," Noah laughed. "But when I got here the nurse let me know where Trixie's room was and that her *brother* was in with her."

Jamie gently placed Trixie's hand back down and grinned slightly. "I knew they'd only let family in with her. I wanted to know her condition."

"I completely understand," Noah nodded. "I've looked the other way plenty of times in these situations. If you care about someone you deserve to know how they are doing."

Jamie nodded his agreement. "The guy who did this . . ." he started as he balled his hands into fists. "He's tied up in some motel room fifteen minutes from here. The police were in here asking what happened, and I told them where they could find him."

"That's good," Noah said tentatively, looking like he knew that wasn't something to rejoice about.

"They'll get a phone call at some point from some higher-up, and they'll cut the guy loose. I should have killed him when I had the chance."

"I can't imagine after a situation like this they'd just let him go. It wouldn't matter who he knows," Noah reasoned.

"I get the impression he's done worse before and got off. I could have ended this, and I didn't." Jamie bit the inside of his cheek as though he were punishing himself.

"I've held a lot of lives in my hands, Jamie. Quite literally. There was this man who came through my ER one night and he'd just murdered his wife and her sister. The police had shot him, and I had my finger plugging up one of his arteries. If I let go, he'd have bled out and died right there."

"What did you do?" Jamie asked, narrowing his eyes at him.

"My job. I saved his life. He went on to get acquitted of the crime because of a technicality. Four months later he killed someone while driving drunk."

"You should have let him die on your table," Jamie said. Noah had a look on his face like he disagreed, but everything he was saying made Jamie's point.

"So now what?" Jamie asked, leaning back in the chair and rubbing at his eyes.

"I'll go grab you something to eat and talk to the nurses about getting a cot for you."

"I'm not hungry or tired." Jamie fought the yawn that crept up the back of his throat.

"Your adrenaline is telling you that. You can do what you want. But my suggestion is you eat, sleep, and take care of yourself so that when she wakes up you're at your best. She'll need you to be at one hundred percent."

Jamie didn't answer. He only shrugged and rolled the tension out of his sore neck. Noah obviously took that as agreement and headed out of the room to do what he had offered.

When the room was quiet again, Jamie's eyes rose and settled on Trixie's battered face. He wasn't sure how he could eat, considering he was sure he'd be sick any minute. At least he could blame it on a stomach bug from Maisie instead of the deep pit of rage and anxiety that was swirling inside him.

A few minutes later a nurse came into the room and checked on Trixie. Jamie recognized her from when he first arrived at the hospital, and a flash of a memory came back to him.

"I think I might have been a jackass to you when we got here," he recalled.

"That's no problem," she said through a sweet smile. "My grandma used to tell me that sometimes being afraid comes out more like being angry. I've learned to tell the difference." She finished the rest of her duties in silence and slipped away before Jamie could properly apologize. He considered going after her and telling her again that he hadn't meant to shout at her. But nothing would take him out of this room. Everything else in the world would have to wait.

CHAPTER TWENTY-SIX

Autumn and Travis sat glued to the television as every news station broadcasted the same thing. Roberta Silverstone was poised with her chin pointed toward the sky behind a podium in front of dozens of cameras. Her hair had enough hairspray to make it resemble a helmet. She cleared her throat, and the entire audience fell dead silent.

"I appreciate you all coming here today. We've already covered the spelling of my name and my credentials. So let's get on with it." She glanced at the stack of papers on the podium in front of her, but Autumn could tell she didn't need them. Raising her head again, she stared directly into the camera. "I'm here today to talk to all of you about corruption. It erodes the very foundation this country was built upon. When it occurs at the highest levels of our government we are forced to pursue justice through more unique channels. That's why I'm here with you today. Evidence came across my desk that a United States senator was involved in the cover-up of criminal behavior."

Roberta paused when a bit of chatter erupted but settled

quickly. "There is a process for this offense, but the deeper I investigated the more apparent it became that I must immediately make this public. The depth of this corruption makes it impossible to safely and effectively pursue justice. With that in mind, I am coming to the members of the media today to help document this situation and bring attention to the grave misuse of power." Roberta braced her hands firmly on the podium, as her voice grew stronger.

"Nevada Senator Clive Strauss . . ." she said, pausing clearly for effect, "has been accused by multiple parties of charges that include conspiracy, bribery, and fraud. I believe with the evidence I have seen so far there will be no delay in an indictment on federal charges. Anyone who holds a seat in the United States Senate should be expected to hold themselves to the highest standard, but these accusations are even more troublesome considering Senator Strauss is a high-ranking member of the Foreign Arms Committee as well as the Appropriations Committee. As many of you know, that puts him in a position of great power in this country, and unfortunately, he has abused that power." She banged her hand against the podium.

"Right now the former girlfriend of Senator Strauss's son is lying in a hospital bed, fighting for her life. She and her young daughter have suffered abuse at the hands of Eli Strauss for more than three years. This alone has been enough to call for justice, but the system has failed them completely. Every time they sought help, or the police were involved, Senator Strauss pulled strings to make the situation disappear. He's trapped this woman and her small daughter in the lair of a beast by trading favors and abusing his power. Through fear and intimidation these two men have manipulated the public. I am here today to plead with the powers of this government to investigate this to the fullest. I have a mountain of paperwork, a laundry list of statements, and a line of witnesses ready to stand together to take this man down. These brave people, willing to stand up and speak the truth, include doctors, nurses, a United States Marshal, security guards, and even some military personnel.

"If you are in a position of power please stand with us. If you are a member of the public, please pray for the woman's recovery." Roberta bowed her head and drew in a deep breath. "I'm sure I'll be slandered and attacked for this. I can bet the victims will be as well. For those of you concerned with the validity of these accusations, this is not a witch-hunt; it is a call for the end of corruption and abuse of power. A call I hope all of you will answer." She stepped back, grabbed her papers, and walked off the stage.

Autumn was astonished, and she smiled when she saw Travis looking exactly the same way. "I don't think I've ever seen anything like that in my life."

"People are going to lose their minds over this. I can only imagine what the news networks are doing right now. Probably scrambling around like chickens with their heads cut off." Travis fiddled with the juice box he'd been holding for the last five minutes and finally remembered to take it to Maisie. When he came back Autumn was still staring at the television as if something else was about to happen.

"She's doing much better," Travis reported as he sidled up next to Autumn and rubbed her back affectionately.

"I hope Trixie is as well," Autumn sighed, thinking of the vibrant woman who had sat in her living room just a few days ago. Now she was in a hospital bed with a brain injury and no guarantee she'd wake up.

"Last update from Jamie was the same. She's still in a medically induced coma, but they're happy to report no further brain swelling. Noah is still there. Jamie had kind of an attitude about it, but I could tell he was glad for the company."

Autumn rested her head on his shoulder and took comfort in his sturdy frame. "That sounds like Jamie," she laughed. "I can't believe all this happened. He's really stepped up for her. I'm just sorry it had to be under these circumstances."

"Me too," Travis agreed. "If any three people deserve to be happy and catch a break it's Jamie, Trixie, and Maisie. I just hope they get their chance."

"What do we do now?" Autumn asked, looking into his face, anxious for some direction.

"If you were four, you just got over being sick, you were worried about your mom, and you were in a strange place, what would you want to do?" Travis asked, the wheels in his mind turning.

"Cry?" Autumn answered honestly.

"We should do something fun. Something that takes her mind off everything." Travis scrolled through his phone as though an answer might pop up there. "What are those dolls little girls like? The ones where they can get clothes, and they all have those weird back-stories. You can go have tea parties and stuff."

"Weird back stories? Umm . . . they're brilliant. They're the best dolls that ever existed, and if you make fun of them, you'll have me to deal with." Autumn shoved away from him and gave him a funny glare.

"So you've heard of them. Then I suppose you know exactly where we can get one?" Travis grabbed his keys off the counter.

"I may receive coupons and a catalog from time to time through my membership to the lifetime fan club." She blushed and rolled her eyes.

"Then I guess you're both in for a fun day." Travis winked and his gentle smile warmed Autumn's heart.

CHAPTER TWENTY-SEVEN

Noah slid another Styrofoam cup of coffee toward Jamie. It was bitter, burnt sludge but he couldn't turn it down. Though he'd dozed off a few times, he hadn't gotten any real sleep, and he didn't want to.

"Her last CT looks good," Noah reported. "No additional bleeding. They've begun weaning her off the sedation medication. Her response will be very telling." Noah sunk back into the chair and shifted uncomfortably.

"You really don't need to stay," Jamie said half-heartedly. If he were being honest with himself, having Noah around was actually helpful. When the doctors and nurses were hard to track down or quick to leave the room, Noah could explain what was coming next.

"And you really don't need to keep saying that. I'm sticking around." Noah sipped at his coffee and winced at the quality.

"You're missing your big trip. Are you sure you aren't just using this as an excuse to chicken out?" Jamie shot a sideways glance at Noah.

"What a way with words you have. You remind me so much of myself. Don't take that as a compliment though. It hasn't gotten me very far."

"You're a doctor," Jamie scoffed. "You must not be doing too bad for yourself. Well, before your wife died, and you went all nuts."

"I was keeping people alive but barely living myself. Things weren't great before my wife died, but they fell apart after. I was angry and tearing down anything I could get my hands on. That sound familiar?"

"Are you trying to diagnose me with something? I don't need my head shrunk." Jamie swigged back half the coffee and rubbed at his tired eyes.

"We just seem a lot alike. I was wondering if you have been as destructive as I've been. Maybe I'm hung up on this introspective stuff. I'm trying to see things differently and remembering everything my wife used to say I ignored." Noah stretched his back again against the rigid chair.

"If I have had a streak of self-destructiveness and now want to stop being a selfish ass and ruining everything I touch . . . what would your wife had told me to do?"

Noah bit at his lip as he thought this through. "My parents weren't particularly warm people," Noah began. "Rayanne came to a few holiday dinners, and it was always so hard for her to understand them. Her family was big hugs and thoughtful gifts. My parents were the opposite. She and my father got in this debate one Thanksgiving about how showing affection wasn't a sign of weakness, like my father was trying to argue. He listed dozens of points about sheltered and coddled children ruining the world. My father believed it was better to face life with the knowledge that everything is temporary. Everyone will die or leave, and showering someone with love or affection is futile. It's a waste of energy. My wife stood up from the table, gently placed her napkin down on her plate, and proceeded to call my father a pitiful excuse for a human. I'll never forget her argument. She looked him square in the eye, which hardly anyone ever did, propped her hands up on her hips, and said, I refuse to live my life pushing people away just because I will lose them someday or they'll lose me. As a matter of fact, I love them like I'm going to lose them any second." Noah spun his wedding ring around on his finger absentmindedly. "After that I told her not to bother to argue with my father. It was pointless. What I should have done was back her up. They were both saying the same thing: life is fragile and you're going to lose people you love. The difference was my father believed that meant there was no point getting attached. Rayanne believed that was the exact reason you should get attached to people, as many as you can. So I think that's the advice she'd give you."

"Damn," Jamie said, raising his eyebrows nearly to his hairline. "People are going to leave you; love them as if they're leaving tomorrow. That's not really the philosophy I've been going by."

"What's yours?" Noah asked.

"People are going to leave you so be such a dick they don't bother sticking around at all. Trixie though," he said, brushing her bangs away from her face, "didn't care what I was saying. It was like she could see through me. She'd forgive me for the dumb crap before I ever said I was sorry."

"That's how Rayanne always was with me," Noah

explained. "I don't think any other woman in the world would know how to deal with me the way she did."

"I think Trixie is the same for me," Jamie said, lowering his head as the realization hit him. He may never have a chance to find out what a future with her would be like.

"They'll be reducing her meds even further soon. She'll be awake, and you'll be able to tell her all that." Noah stood up, the rigid chair winning the battle against comfort.

"You think she can hear me now, though?" Jamie asked, searching Noah's face for any sign of a lie.

"I do," he said confidently. "There is some science to back it up as well. The brain is a mysterious thing. I believe talking to her now is important." Noah took that as a cue to leave and headed into the hallway.

Jamie took Trixie's hand in his and kissed her knuckles. "Trix," he began but stopped suddenly when he felt emotion gurgling up the back of his throat. He forced composure and continued, "I want you to know something. No matter what happens to you, Maisie will be safe. I will make sure of that. She'll know everything there is to know about her mother and the bravery it took to face what you did. She will never be alone. I promise you." His voice shook. "And I want you to know I've never loved anyone. I've never even liked myself. But y-you . . ." he stuttered. "It's easy being around you. I don't have to change or apologize. I'm not pretending. I think I could be with you for a long time. I hope I get to."

Her hand twitched in his then squeezed. It was fleeting. So much so he couldn't tell if it had really happened or he'd just wished it to be true. "Trixie," he said quietly. When her eyelids fluttered, his voice grew louder. Loud enough to draw Noah in from the hallway.

"What's going on?" he called and made his way to the side of her bed.

"I think she's waking up. Her hand moved and then her eyes. Should she be waking up already?" Jamie felt like his heart might pop in his chest, but he couldn't decide if it was from worry or relief.

"She's heavily medicated, but she might be fighting hard to get out of it. Hit the nurse call button. Trixie, if you can hear me, I want you to try to stay calm. You're intubated with a breathing tube and that can feel very strange, but try to lie still. The nurse will be here in a moment."

Noah seemed perfectly prepared for Trixie to ignore his suggestion. And she did. With the little energy she had, she writhed up and down, turning her head from side to side. Noah tried to brace her shoulders. "Talk to her Jamie, calm her down."

"I—umm, I'm not sure," Jamie started, but Noah cut in angrily.

"Jamie, she could injure herself further. Say something to calm her down."

He leaned over her body, ignoring the tears rolling down her cheeks and falling onto the bandages wrapped around her head. "Maisie is okay," Jamie stuttered out. "She's safe. You saved her life by locking her in the car. I found her soon after. She's with Travis and Autumn, and she's just fine."

"You hear that Trixie?" Noah asked as a few nurses came thundering into the room. "You are safe in the hospital. Lie still."

The nurse injected something into Trixie's IV, and a few seconds later she was lying still again. "She must have really wanted to wake up," the tall thin nurse said as she disposed of the needle. "She should not have been alert with that amount of sedation."

"It's my fault," Jamie said timidly. "I was talking to her and updating her about her daughter. I shouldn't have done that."

"Waking up is a good thing," comforted one of the nurses. "If she's got that much fight in her and was recognizing your voice, that's very promising."

Jamie nodded as though he felt better, but he didn't. "What happens next? If she's going to be that agitated when she wakes up, how will you do it safely?"

"I'll check with her doctor. Normally though we'd just take it a little slower with us all in here. You were doing the right thing. Talking to her and instructing her to be still and calm is a great start." She patted his shoulder on her way out the door, and he forced a smile.

"I know it's hard, Jamie," Noah sighed. "I think it's part of the reason I was so shut off from people. All those years working I never let myself really understand how difficult it was to watch someone you love struggle. It's hard. I can finally see that." He clasped a hand down on Jamie's shoulder. In the past Jamie would have shrugged it off, but he let it stay. It kept him from falling forward and smacking his face down on the hard tile floor.

"I want Travis," Jamie croaked. "I know he's helping with Maisie and everything, but I want him here. Maybe they should all come and stay close by. Maisie could come see her at some point right?"

"You'll know when the time is right for that."

Jamie looked over at Trixie, trails of tears still streaked

down her face. The time wasn't right yet; he knew that. She wouldn't want her daughter seeing her like this.

"The doctor will be by soon to give you an update," Noah explained.

"Hang out here, will you?" Jamie asked, clearing his throat to strengthen his voice. He knew he was sounding weak, like a little kid looking for someone to back him up.

"Yeah," Noah said, shrugging like it was no big deal. "I'm not going anywhere."

CHAPTER TWENTY-EIGHT

"We'll stay in a hotel there?" Autumn asked, watching Travis rummage through the bag he'd hastily packed.

"I guess so. I haven't really thought that far ahead. If you heard the way Jamie sounded on the phone you'd understand why I'm in such a rush. He was beside himself. I've never heard him like that before. He asked me to come."

"Maisie is finally settled in here," Autumn said, trying to picture the little girl hanging out all day in a hotel room waiting for her mom to be better. Something that might not even happen. "I'm not sure it's a great idea."

"Autumn," Travis said with a look like she'd just slapped him. "I have to go. Jamie asked me to come, and I'm not going to leave him hanging like that."

"I'm not suggesting you should. I'm saying she shouldn't go. It doesn't sound like Trixie is in good enough shape yet. I don't think Maisie should see her like that."

"We'll wait until Trixie is doing better before she visits," Travis countered, sounding far more defensive than Autumn expected.

"But what is she going to do in a hotel all day besides worry about her mom? At least here Donna can come by and visit. She has some dolls to play with. I can wash her clothes here. It makes sense for her to stay." Autumn spoke gently, trying to keep Travis calm enough to actually think this through.

"And you'll stay with her here? You're fine with that?" he asked, his face finally softening to the idea.

"We'll figure it out." She shrugged. "We have our cool dolls to play with. I'm sure we'll be fine. You should go. Jamie needs you. But I think Maisie needs to stay here. We should divide and conquer."

Travis opened his mouth to make another argument, but Autumn could tell he actually agreed with her. "Jamie wanted her to come, but maybe it's not a great idea. He'll probably be pissed at the change of plans. But if she's doing well here, she should stay." He worked through every angle in his mind and each turn showed on his face.

"Go," Autumn said, making the choice for him. "Get down there. Be with him. He needs you. I'll hold down the fort here."

He pulled his bag over his shoulder and moved toward her. She expected a hug, maybe a peck on the cheek to say goodbye. Instead he kissed her full on the lips. It wasn't passionate or hungry; it was slow and warm. It was a connection, like hearing a song for the first time and realizing it would someday be one of your favorites.

"I'm sorry," he said as he pulled away, his hand still resting on her cheek. "I'm just grateful to have you. Not only have you been understanding with all of this, you also keep helping every chance you get. I've been alone for so long I forgot how nice it is to be part of a team."

"Don't apologize," she said, waving him off. "I'm happy to help, and that," she said, touching her lips gently, "was really nice. I forgot how nice it could be." She slid her arms around his waist and tucked her head against his chest.

Kissing the top of her head, he pulled away again. "Say goodbye to Maisie for me."

He was out the door and down the driveway before Autumn could even whisper goodbye. Here she was being kissed for the first time in a long time, charged with the care of a four-year-old, and her fridge was pretty much bare.

"Maisie," she called into the other room, "do you like the grocery store?" If the little girl answered yes, that would make one of them. Autumn had been using a grocery delivery service since Charlie had died. She had no desire to do that chore anymore. But kids needed food. Probably real food like fruits and vegetables, not just pizza. And if she were being honest with herself, anything that made that little girl smile gave her this jolt of joy. And when everything had been so dark for so long, even a tiny twinkling star was welcome.

CHAPTER TWENTY-NINE

Jamie could tell by the look on Travis's face this was as bad as it seemed. When Travis looked at Trixie, he held his breath and stuttered out his hello.

"She's actually doing better," Jamie tried to explain. "Better than she was when she got here anyway. They've dialed down the sedation medicine, and she's been lucid a few times. The doctor took the breathing tube out; that should help a lot. She was talking a little bit about an hour ago."

"Good," Travis said, his eyes still fixed on Trixie and the machines surrounding her. "How are you? Have you eaten or slept?"

"Noah's been all over me about that junk," Jamie said with the familiar roll of his eyes. "I'm good. Where are Autumn and Maisie; did you find a hotel?"

"Umm," Travis finally turned his attention to Jamie, "they didn't come."

"What do you mean they didn't come?" he asked, tilting his head in confusion.

"She's doing really well at Autumn's house," Travis explained. "Look at this." He cued up a picture on his phone and spun it so Jamie could see. "They're baking cookies. Doesn't she look happy?"

"Since when can Autumn bake?" Jamie asked, scrutinizing the picture.

"They are the ones you just break apart and bake, but still they're doing great. Maisie has been uprooted enough. She needs something steady right now."

"Is Autumn steady?" Jamie asked with one eyebrow cocked up. "She was doing better than when we met her, but she still had some bad days."

"Autumn has it completely under control now. I actually think having Maisie there is helping a lot. That little girl has an infectious smile."

"Yes she does," Trixie said in a hoarse whisper that sounded like her throat was full of nails.

"Trix," Jamie said, racing toward her bedside again. "How are you doing? Are you in any pain?"

"My head is killing me," she breathed out and reached a hand up to touch it, but Jamie stopped her just in time.

"You had surgery. You can't touch the bandages," he explained gently. "You're all right though. Everything is going to be fine."

"Maisie?" she asked, a flash of panic blazing across her face.

"She's with Autumn," Travis cut in. "They're baking cookies and playing dolls. She's thinking of you of course, but she's thoroughly distracted right now."

Trixie nodded her head but stopped abruptly when the pain seemed to return sharply.

"Just lie still," Jamie insisted and hit the nurses' call button. "They'll give you more pain meds."

"I don't want to be knocked out again," she moaned. "I want to know what's going on." She was making her case, but pain was written all over her face.

"Excuse me," an unfamiliar man said as he peeked his head in the door. He wasn't in scrubs or a doctor's coat, so Jamie's antennas went right up.

"Who are you?" he asked, blocking the man from coming in any farther.

"My name is Drake Telusa. I'm here on behalf of the United States Attorney General, as the appointed head of the task force spearheading the investigation of Senator Clive Strauss."

"Get the hell out of here," Jamie insisted, puffing his chest at the tall, wide-shouldered man with a crew cut and business suit.

"Jamie, wait," Travis interrupted, putting one hand on his chest and pushing him back slightly. "I've heard of this guy. You were the one who pulled off that racketeering conviction in Boston a couple of years ago."

"It was one of the largest in history," he said proudly, still waiting to be let into the room. "And my father did the same in his day back in Chicago. I just went into the family business."

His smile was meant to be disarming, but to Jamie it was arrogant. "Now's not the time," Jamie spat out, inching his way forward again, even with Travis's palm planted on his chest.

"Now is the only time, actually. I'm your golden ticket right now. Anything Trixie needs we hash it out now, and I get to work." Drake nudged his way into the room and Travis let him pass, holding Jamie back.

"She doesn't need anything from you. The only thing she needs is time to heal." Jamie moved his body between Drake and Trixie so he couldn't get a good look at her and she wouldn't be disturbed by him.

"We're talking about the indictment of a United States senator that sits on some of the most powerful committees in our government. He's a mob boss with a fancy title, and he's not going to take this lying down. I can offer Trixie protection for herself and anyone else who may need it. I can arrange for her care while she heals. And more importantly, I can ensure her daughter is cared for."

"Her daughter is fine," Jamie bit back.

"I have no doubt she is, but with Trixie incapacitated and the little girl's father deceased years ago, she'll need a guardian."

"I want her with Travis and Autumn," Trixie said, forcing the words through her dry lips.

Drake sidestepped Jamie and moved closer to her. "I can draft up a temporary custody agreement that names them as her guardians," he offered. "If that's what you want, I can take care of that for you."

"Yes," she said through strained lips.

"Then consider it done," Drake assured her.

"She needs pain medication," Travis reminded Jamie, who finally stepped into the hallway and started yelling until a nurse came running. Within a minute Trixie was sedated again, sleeping through the rest of the conversation.

"I may have made an incorrect assumption there," Drake admitted. "I should have asked if you and Autumn are offering to care for the girl. Also there may need to be a home study to make sure the arrangement works in the eyes of the state, but I didn't feel it was necessary to trouble Trixie with those worries."

"I'm a licensed foster parent already. I was his, actually," Travis explained, pointing at Jamie. "But don't let that be a reflection on me. He was screwed up before I got him." Travis smirked at Jamie who could only huff and roll his eyes.

"That will help the process greatly. And you and Autumn are agreeing to care for her, correct?"

"Yes," Travis said without hesitation, and Jamie had to fight the lump that grew in his throat. The gratitude he felt for this man took up space in his body where air should be.

"If, for some reason, and I know this isn't likely, Trixie does not recover to where she can care for her daughter, would you be willing to take on a more permanent roll?"

"Like adoption?" Travis asked, stuttering on the word. "I mean, I can't speak for Autumn. That's a conversation she'd need to weigh in on. But for me," Travis said, scratching his head nervously, "yes, if Trixie couldn't care for Maisie, I would adopt her."

"Great, we're making good progress here," Drake explained. "I'll get those documents drafted and ready for you and Autumn to sign. I'll just need your personal information. You can email it to me here." He passed him a business card and kept speaking so quickly Jamie had to fight to keep up. "I'll also need a list from you, regarding who, besides Trixie and her daughter, might need security assigned to them. We have a great team, and the number of men and women are limitless so if you think someone may be affected, put them on the list. When I've dealt with this level of corruption in the past I've always been shocked how far and deep it reaches. As well as what men are willing to do to keep themselves from prosecution."

"My mother," Jamie croaked out. "She's institutionalized in California. I think that might be information that Eli or Clive have. She'd be afraid of any kind of security, but I'd want to know she was safe."

"Put her on the list," Drake insisted. "My men can be sensitive to the situation."

"What exactly is the status of the investigation? I know the local police picked up Eli and probably filed a report about Trixie's abduction." Travis always asked the right questions at just the right time. Another thing Jamie was grateful for.

Drake slid his bag off his shoulder and started digging through it. "Eli has been moved to a secure location. We didn't want to take any risks with a local precinct being persuaded to let him go or anything. He isn't going anywhere now. We have footage of him abducting Trixie. At some point we'll have her statement to back it up. Plus the supplies in his car make a pretty good case for what he had in mind for Trixie."

"What do you mean?" Jamie asked, feeling a prickly heat of anger roll up his spine.

"He had handcuffs, a shovel, duct tape, some acid. It was like a goody bag for a serial killer." Drake said this casually, but it sent Jamie into a rage.

"This guy is going to keep getting off. It doesn't matter where you move him, or what you think you're capable of. I should have taken care of him when I had a chance." Jamie slammed his hand down on the rolling table next to Trixie's bed.

"Eli will never see the light of day again. He's done. I've gotten a look at Roberta Silverstone's investigation and witness statements. She has all her ducks in a row. I'm coming in to give her some support, but I'll tell you, she hardly needs it. That woman is frighteningly good. I think there will be an indictment for the senator by the end of the week."

"You'll have to forgive me if I don't hold my breath. I hope you're right, but I don't put anything past these guys. They are capable of anything."

"Roberta has a U.S. Marshal claiming to know this family's secrets. He's willing to talk, and rumor has it that's because of you," Drake said, posing it as more of a question.

"I needed information from him, and he sounded like a guy who was looking for a way out. I wasn't even sure Roberta would want anything to do with him. He actually helped me find Trixie, so I hope it works out for him."

"He's going to make out just fine. His family is already in protective custody, and he's in the process of trading his sworn statement for immunity. If he can stay out of the senator's crosshairs he might actually be able to salvage his life." Drake looked at a few of his notes and finally took a seat. "Now, I need your statement, Jamie. Tell me anything you witnessed, anything Trixie told you during your time together. No detail is too small." His pen hovered over the paper while he waited for Jamie to start, but he didn't.

How was he supposed to relive every moment he had with Trixie without wanting to explode? Would she ever be the same? Would they be able to pick up where they left off?

The questions swirled like water disappearing down a drain. "I don't really want to rehash all of it," Jamie grunted.

"We're on a very tight schedule," Drake explained as he tapped his pen to the paper a few times. "Roberta and I are meeting with the attorney general in the morning. There will be leadership there from the FBI, and we want to get the senator in front of a federal court as soon as possible. I'm telling you all of this so you can see there are not only a lot of moving parts but they're moving at lightning speed. Never has a senator in such a high-ranking position been accused of so many charges."

"So when does he go to jail?" Jamie asked, jumping to the bottom line.

"That can be tricky. There is no actual law or rule that says he has to step down from his job in the Senate just because he's been indicted on charges like corruption or conspiracy. I know that sounds crazy, but it's true. He'll go through a trial and the outcome of that will determine his jail time, if any. From what I've seen of the case Roberta has built so far, the justice department might find charges beyond those that are deemed criminal, and then he could be held without bail if the court determines it is warranted."

"Of course he's done criminal things," Jamie said, annoyed by the lack of confidence Drake was offering.

"He's violated his post for sure. He's made backroom deals, bribed people, taken campaign funds he shouldn't have, and intimidated folks into hiding his son's crimes. The list goes on, but if he hasn't committed a crime like assault or kidnapping like Eli did, then it would be difficult for him to be held without bail. But getting absolutely everything documented is what we need today. That's why I need your statement. Getting Trixie's would be important too. I can stick around until that latest dose of pain meds wears off."

"She's in a lot of pain. You can't grill her and push her right now," Jamie argued. "You'll have to make do without her statement."

"Is that what she would want?" Drake asked, glancing over at Trixie. He moved in closer and rested a hand on her still shoulder. Leaning down, he whispered quietly, "That son of a bitch is going to get everything he deserves. You're safe now."

"I don't want to talk in here," Jamie said, folding his arms across his chest. "I don't want her hearing it all dredged up again. She doesn't need that."

Drake nodded his agreement and gathered up his things, shoving them into his bag. "How about a soggy Caesar salad and some stale chips from the cafeteria?"

"You'll stay with her?" Jamie asked Travis, who'd uncharacteristically managed not to butt in to the conversation even though he likely had a strong opinion.

"Of course," he assured Jamie.

"Noah should be back in a little while too. He went to get some sleep and a shower. Once he gets here, if you want to take off or whatever . . ." Jamie shrugged.

"I'm going to be right here," Travis insisted, gesturing at the chair he was sitting in. "She won't be alone for a second."

CHAPTER THIRTY

Two weeks could feel like two years when your entire life hangs in the balance. Jamie had lost track of what day of the week it was, but he was pretty sure, judging by the nursing staff that had just rotated in, it was Friday night.

"Hey, Amy," Jamie said, waving at the dark-skinned nurse who he'd spent hours chatting with over the weeks. He knew about her sick cat and her husband's promising job offer.

"How's it going, Jamie?" she asked as she tiptoed into the room and checked Trixie's vital signs.

"Pretty good. She's had a great day. Physical therapy isn't her favorite, but she's showing improvement."

"I've been watching the news closely," she said as she took a seat next to him. Her shift hadn't even started yet. This was a social visit more than anything. Jamie hadn't spent much time in a hospital, but apparently if you do, you become part of the inner circle. "It looks like the senator doesn't stand a chance. All his supporters are backing down, and they're calling for him to step down. I have no idea how he's made it this far without making a statement or anything."

"Drake thinks that's a good sign," Jamie explained. "If he had anything worth saying he'd have done it by now. He must know it's over. The only thing I wish is that he was in jail already. It blows my mind that a man can break so many laws and still be walking the streets. That doesn't seem like justice."

"But Eli is locked up and that's good," she countered. Amy was a glass half full kind of woman, and while that personality used to annoy Jamie, now he found it refreshing. He couldn't figure out how to be that way himself, but he could appreciate it when he heard it from someone else.

"It shows his father's power is gone. No more calling in a favor and springing him from jail. Roberta would stand outside his cell herself if she had to. She's not letting him go anywhere." Jamie quieted abruptly as Trixie began to stir.

"Hey girl," Amy said with a beaming smile. "How are you feeling?"

"I'm really sick of waking up in this place," she admitted with a sigh. "I was just dreaming of being at the park with Maisie."

Jamie wanted to ask if he was in the dream as well. He'd never been one to need any kind of reassurance of his worth. His ego was a self-sustaining machine. But part of him had imagined when Trixie woke up and started talking more frequently, she'd have some deep professions of love and dreams of the future. But she hadn't. She'd wanted frequent updates on Maisie, of course. She wanted to know absolutely everything as it happened with Clive and Eli Strauss. There was always talk about her progress and prognoses. When all that was done there never seemed enough time or energy to ask what the future held for the two of them.

"You'll be pushing her on the swing before you know it," Amy chirped optimistically. "I've got to go clock in. You should try to get some rest. If you need something to help you sleep just hit the call button."

When Amy slipped out, the room quieted around them again. Jamie didn't want to keep Trixie up with useless chatter. But every time he looked at her she was wide awake, staring at the ceiling.

"I know you're sick of this place," Jamie commiserated. "But it's important you sleep. Do you want Amy to bring you something?"

"No," she said curtly. "Why are you still here, Jamie?" she asked, narrowing her eyes at him as though she were trying to see into his mind.

"What do you mean? I've been here the whole time."

"I know. You've been sleeping in that damn chair, eating terrible cafeteria food, and acting like you've got nowhere better to be, even though we both know you do." Trixie put a hand up to her forehead and then brought it down over her eyes.

"Are you having head pain?" he asked, misjudging the motion as something other than frustration.

"No, please stop trying to be my nurse. This isn't you. I don't need you acting like you don't want to run the hell out of here the first chance you get. I can't even hold a pen right now, Jamie. I can't get myself back and forth to the bathroom. I have no idea what type of life I'm going to have after this. Can I hold my daughter? Can I push her on that swing?" The tears were streaming down her face now, and her anger was boiling over. Jamie felt the fight or flight sensation he'd lived with most of his life creep up his back. But he shook it off.

"I'm not going anywhere, Trixie. There isn't anywhere else I want to be." He kept his voice level and considered sitting by her bed and holding her hand, but her body language was still too rigid.

"Shut up," she said, punctuating it with a furious laugh. "You want to be in a hospital room right now on some uncomfortable chair, waiting to see if I'm ever going to get better? This is exactly where you want to be? Don't you hear me? I don't know what I can even do. What I'll ever be able to do."

"Where is this coming from? I've been here the whole time. I haven't said anything about wanting to leave."

"Jamie, you should just go. Please. I don't want you here looking at me like this anymore. You aren't the guy who deals with this kind of stuff. Go back to the casino. Win some more money and go travel like you wanted to. You didn't sign up for this. These are my mistakes. I have to live with the consequences."

Jamie had never worked so hard to control his words. His instinct was to scream at her. How dare she tell him he should go? After all he'd done for her. He'd sat vigil by her bed. He'd encouraged and protected her. How dare she? But he knew better. Looking at her now was like looking at himself in the mirror. Telling someone to leave, pushing someone as hard as you could, demanding they fail you, was language he was fluent in. But he'd never been on this side of it. Was this how Travis felt every time he'd told him to go to hell? To leave him alone? To stop showing up? It hurt more than he realized.

"Trixie," Jamie said in a level voice, "I'm sorry this

happened to you. You can blame yourself if you want, but I don't blame you. If you look at what's happening to them now, you'll see that the only people to blame are Clive and Eli. You may have walked into the trap, but they are the ones who set it."

She didn't reply with words, just an angry glare and the shaking of her head.

"And I don't know what your life is going to be like after this. Maybe you won't get any better than you are right now. Maybe this will be the best you ever are. But I'm not leaving. I love you." He didn't stutter a bit, even though the words were not something he often said. "If you can't push Maisie on the swing, I will. If you can't pick up a pen, I'll write down anything you need. Maybe I wasn't always this guy. Maybe I've let a lot of people down. But I am not going to let you down. I am not going to let Maisie down. You get to be angry with the world right now." There was something Travis had said to him not long after he'd first gone to live with him that rang in his ears. Goosebumps spread across his body as he said it out loud. "I'd rather be your punching bag right now than not be in your life. I love you, and that's still the truth, even if you don't love me. I don't need you to. I can wait until you do."

She sobbed as someone does when they have no control: body shaking, whimpering kind of cry that just has to come out so you don't explode. "Jamie," she croaked out, opening her arms and shifting in the bed so that he could lie beside her.

"I'm here," he whispered into her ear as he crawled in beside her.

"I do love you," she cried. "I'm just so scared."

"Well I'm not," he said, squeezing her against his body. "The only thing that scared me was the thought of not finding you. Now you're here. Maisie is safe. Nothing else in the world matters to me."

"I don't know what my life will be like," she sniffled.

"You will be Maisie's mom. You will love her and teach her exactly what she needs to know about life. There will be adventures, vacations, and picnics."

"And you'll be there? Even when it's hard and even when I screw up?" Trixie asked, her head pressed against his chest as though she were speaking right to his heart.

"I'll be there," he promised. "I'm sure I'll screw things up too. It's kind of my thing. But I'll stick with you if you'll stick with me."

Jamie reached into his pocket and pulled out something he'd intended to hold on to until she was released from the hospital. It was going to be celebratory and a fresh start. But he was learning that starting over could be something you did again and again. It didn't have to wait for the perfect moment.

"Marry me," he said, tucking the small diamond ring into her palm. "Marry me and promise to deal with me forever. I'll promise to put up with you too."

"That's crazy," she said, not even looking at the ring before she pushed it back toward him. "Too many things are up in the air to be engaged right now."

"I'll love you no matter what works out and what doesn't. Nothing is going to change tomorrow or the next day for me. Marry me." He pushed the ring back toward her and moved off the bed and down on one knee. "If you were waiting for me to beg . . ." He smiled.

"You don't need to beg," she said, putting her hand out so

he could slide the ring on. "It's beautiful." She blinked away stray tears. "Travis is going to flip out, don't you think? He'll say we're rushing things and we're crazy."

"I doubt it," Jamie laughed at the irony. "It's his wife's ring. He brought it down here two days ago when I told him I was going to propose." He stood again and kissed her head where the bandages were still thickly wrapped.

"Thank you for finding me that night on the side of the road. Somehow I knew you would. Even when it got dark and I was alone, I knew you would find me."

"I spent five years on the side of a dark road myself," Jamie admitted. "You found me first."

CHAPTER THIRTY-ONE

This was long overdue, or at least that's what Trixie kept telling him. As he stood in the lobby of the Sunny Creek Mental Institution he felt like he might be sick. It was nothing like he'd pictured it. He assumed it would be something out of an old horror movie with gray walls and crazy people, rocking away in the corners. It was bright and felt more like a hotel lobby. He was greeted by a beautiful older woman whose nametag read Flo. She pointed him in the direction of his mother's room, and though he thanked her, he never moved.

He questioned again why he agreed to come and looked at his phone to reread the text message from Trixie. She'd sent it for this very moment, telling him when he was thinking about bailing he should read it.

This is a part of us becoming the best people we can be for Maisie and each other.

She was right, if Jamie kept spending a portion of his time wondering about his mother and holding so much hate for her, then it would be space he couldn't give to Trixie and

Maisie. Just like when Trixie sat in front of a grand jury and told her story of abuse and her abduction. It wasn't easy, but it was the stone she'd have to step on in order to cross the river where Jamie was waiting.

"Your mother is a lovely woman," Flo said as she gently touched Jamie's shoulder. "I've worked here for the last three years and have spent a lot of time with her. She talks about you often, but to be honest, I wasn't sure if you were real or not."

"I'm real," he said, drawing in a deep breath.

"I know mental illness can be scary. You never know which version of someone you may get. But your mother has far more good days than bad. I think today is one of the good ones."

Jamie stepped forward, not because he was ready to see his mom, but because he couldn't talk to Flo any longer about her. He meandered down the brightly lit hallways and watched for the room number Flo had given him.

If he had planned a speech or an argument, it evaporated from his mind the moment he saw her reading a book in the rocking chair in the corner of her room. She was still so beautiful. Her hair was long and brown, brushed flat and tamed, unlike the way it used to go wild when she was having a bad day. She didn't notice him right away, and it gave him time to decide whether he should stay or not.

"Mom," he croaked out awkwardly, and she jumped at the sound of his voice. "Mom, it's me, Jamie."

"Oh my gosh," she sang out. "You're a man." She stood so quickly the book in her hands went flying to the ground. "Look how big you are."

"I can't stay long," Jamie lied, putting up the first brick on the protective wall he was building between them.

"I can't believe you came," she said, blinking hard to try to make sure he was real. "You are here, right? This is happening?"

"Yes," he said, pulling back when she reached up for his face.

"Can't I touch you?" she asked, full of sorrow. "I won't know if you're real if I don't touch you."

He leaned toward her reluctantly and let her cold fingers run along his cheek. "Mom, I'm not even sure why I'm here. I just wanted to see how you are, I guess."

"I'm good," she sang out, moving toward her chair and gesturing for him to sit on the edge of her bed. He did so reluctantly, not wanting to look too comfortable. "They take such good care of me here. My son sent lots of money so I could stay, did you know that?"

And in that moment it all came back to him. She could so easily slip between reality and the abyss of her mind where all the confusion lived. He'd been a master at this, years ago. Don't bring attention to the mistake, don't make her feel bad she can't get it right. But things were different now.

"I'm your son. I sent the money." His voice was cold and annoyed. "You'll be able to stay here now. I'll make sure it's always paid for."

"Oh, that's so good," she said, clapping her hands together. "They are very nice to me here. Some of the girls remind me of my daughters. They're in college now you know. So successful."

"Your daughters are in college now?" Jamie asked, feeling

the desire to shake her and scream into her face that her daughters were dead because of her.

"Yes. One will be a doctor, and the other a dentist." She fiddled nervously with her fingers the way she always did when he was growing up. He noticed she didn't say their names. It was something he never brought himself to do either.

"That's great," he agreed, but he couldn't fight off the urge to force her to hear the truth about what had really happened. She'd started a fire. She'd left her little girls to die. "I'm getting married," he said, forcing a change of subject.

"You are?" she asked, covering her mouth with her hands. "When? I'll need time to get a dress."

"You'll have time," he lied. "Her name is Trixie, and she has a little girl named Maisie. She's just turned five."

"You were always so wonderful with your little sisters," she said, and he watched as she disappeared into the past and the sad truth crept in. "You were so good with all of us. I don't know how you did it. How did you ever do it all?"

"I didn't," Jamie huffed. "I failed. I was trying to make it all work, and instead of saving everyone, I ruined everything."

"Oh Jamie," she said, leaning in and touching his cheek again. "You gave me four years with my daughters that I never would have had. You gave me so much joy. What happened wasn't your fault. You were a child. I was the grownup. I belonged in a place like this. You didn't fail us; I failed us."

How, he wondered, did a woman who could barely remember the topic of conversation be able to speak so profoundly about something she'd just denied existed moments earlier?

"You did more than you ever should have had to. I'm sorry you had to. I hope you are happy now. I hope you still have time to be happy."

"I am," Jamie admitted, wiping away a stray tear. "I found some really good people. They care a lot about me. Even before I cared about myself."

"That's so good dear. I knew my kids would be all right. You're getting married, your sisters are in college. It all worked out." She nodded and whispered to herself as she twisted the locket on the necklace she wore.

He let the anger roll off his shoulders. "It did, Mom," he lied. "Everything worked out." It would have been easier to tell her she was wrong. He could remind her of every mistake she'd ever made and all they had lost because of her. It was not hard for him to access that list in his mind. It was one he went over often. But maybe that was the point. Why keep score when it would hurt to relive it? "You did the best you could. We both did." He gave up fighting the tears. They trailed down his cheeks and dropped to the floor.

"You're going to be a great husband. I'm sorry I can't see you get married," she apologized, now seeming to remember that wouldn't be possible. She patted his hand and stood as she began searching for something. "I want to give you this." She pulled a framed picture out of a drawer, and he instantly recognized the family photo his mother had insisted they all had taken one Thanksgiving. Even though they hardly had any money and their clothes were mismatched. But her smile in that picture was one of pride and excitement.

"You keep it, Mom," he insisted, not sure he wanted to look at it. He hadn't seen a photograph of his sisters since their faces appeared in the newspaper to report their death.

"Even if you don't look at it," she said, pushing it toward him, "you should still have it, because one day you might want to look at it." She flipped it over and handed it to him so the back of the frame was all he could see. "I'm so very sorry, Jamie." She looked as though she wasn't exactly sure what to be sorry for, but her words were enough for him. "I was so afraid you'd be too angry to live your life."

"I was," he said with a small laugh, "but some people wouldn't give up on me, no matter how much I begged them to. They saved my life."

"I'd like to thank them someday," she said, searching his face for his reaction.

"Maybe," he shrugged. "I still have to thank them."

"Well, do, because if they helped you be this man, I owe them more than I'll ever be able to repay them." She dropped her head, and he recognized immediately her posture of sadness and heard the familiar sound of her crying. "I really wanted to be better. I wanted to not be sick anymore."

With that one proclamation, something Jamie always knew deep down, he felt a piece of himself dislodge. She didn't choose this life. She didn't ask to be sick, and she'd have traded anything to be better. He could blame her. He could blame himself, but now looking back on it, they never stood a chance. Whatever time they had together, whatever memories didn't hurt, were a blessing. The fact that they had anything at all to hang on to was miraculous.

"I do love you, Mom," he admitted as though he was telling himself for the first time. "I'm sorry you have to be here."

"I love it here," she said as though his statement was

ridiculous. "You know my son just sent a lot of money so I can stay."

With that he stood and smiled at her. "That's such good news." He sighed. "I'm so glad."

"He's a good boy," she said, nodding her head. "He was always a good boy."

He leaned down and kissed her cheek before heading into the hallway. He didn't talk to Flo or anyone else on his way out. He did his best to get back on the road but a couple minutes later had to pull off the road, and he cried until his sides hurt. When he'd call Trixie later he'd tell her it went well, and he was glad he went. That would be true, but he'd leave this part out. He'd leave out the hurt he unleashed from the prison he'd locked it in over the years. He was just glad it was out now. He was glad it made more space in his life for the people who deserved to be there.

CHAPTER THIRTY-TWO

"It's normal for the best man to toast the groom, but today I'd like to turn that around." Jamie stood in front of the small group that had gathered to see Trixie and him exchange vows. They were all barefoot, toes in the sand, watching the waves roll in behind him.

"I never knew my father," he started and immediately choked up, having to shake off the emotion. "I knew this would be hard," he admitted. Travis was already in tears; he had been since he walked Trixie down the aisle. But now he was really blubbering. "I never knew my father," Jamie stared again. "I don't know the man who dated my mother and left us. I'm not sure if he likes football or what color his eyes were. I used to be angry about that. Every kid should know his father. But then I realized something. You might not ever meet your father, but it doesn't mean you can't know your dad. Because a dad isn't the guy who makes up half your DNA. He's the guy who shows up and tells you, well before you're ready to believe him, that everything is going to be all right. He's the guy who chases you down and tells you to straighten up. He's tough love and gentle apologies when he's wrong. I may never know my father. But I am lucky enough to know a man who is Dad. As I find myself in the same position, hoping to be Dad, even though I'm not her father, I hope I'm able to do it the way you did, Travis."

Travis laughed. "Hopefully she's less trouble then you were."

"Oh, let's hope so," Trixie teased as she sidled up to Jamie and wrapped her arms around him. Maisie was at their feet a moment later and pawing to be picked up.

"Family hug," she insisted as she pressed her cheeks to theirs and squeezed them tightly.

When everyone had dunked their feet in the water for the last time and gathered up their things to leave, Travis caught Jamie's arm. He expected to hear some gushy thank you for the toast and a tight hug, but that wasn't it at all.

"I'm going to tell Autumn I love her," he coughed out nervously. "Well, I'm thinking about it anyway. I'm just not sure how she feels. Things are good with us right now. They are slow, and they make sense. Maybe I should just leave well enough alone."

"Are you asking me for advice?" Jamie teased, realizing how far his life had come. Never did he imagine he'd be Travis's source for an opinion. He'd always just been a burden. "She loves you," Jamie said confidently. "It's written all over her face. Whether or not she's ready to put that label on it, who knows? Maybe she misses her husband sometimes, but I think she loves you all the time. She can do both. And you know what, even if she's not ready to say it back, it doesn't mean you shouldn't tell her how you feel. Just don't pressure her."

"That's insightful," Travis said, looking shocked.

"Hey, I've evolved." Jamie threw an elbow into Travis' ribs and smiled. "Autumn," he called out, racing away from Travis before he could stop him, "wait up a bit. Travis wants to talk to you."

"I'm going to kill you," Travis threatened as Autumn headed back toward them.

"Life's too short, Travis," Jamie reminded him. "You have no idea how many days you'll get to tell her you love her. You might as well start that clock today. Get as many of them in as you can."

Jamie left them to talk and ran to catch up with Maisie and Trixie. "You ready for your sleepover at Aunt Autumn and Uncle Travis's?" he asked, lifting Maisie up and putting her on his shoulders.

"Why can't I go with you?" she pouted.

"You get to spend the rest of your life with us," Trixie explained. "Jamie and I want one night here at the beach to celebrate being married."

"Well what are you going to do?" she asked, raising a tiny eyebrow at her mother.

"Read," Trixie blurted out. "We're going to read books."

"It's true," Jamie assured Maisie. "Long books that take all night to read. We're going to read and read and then read some more."

Trixie threw him a look before breaking into a smile. He put Maisie down and she climbed into the back seat.

"Reading?" he teased Trixie when Maisie was out of earshot.

"I panicked," Trixie shrugged.

"I can't believe we're married," he said, leaning down and

kissing her lips passionately. "I can't wait to read to you all night."

"What's taking Autumn and Travis so long?" Trixie asked, standing on her tiptoes to look over his shoulder to see what they were doing.

"He's telling her he loves her," he whispered in her ear. "He wasn't sure if he should, but I told him he'd be crazy not to."

When Trixie broke out laughing, he pulled away to get a better look at her. "She was going to tell him too. She asked me what I thought about it yesterday. I told her the same thing."

"They're good together," Jamie said, wrapping an arm around his wife and watching Autumn and Travis smile as they spoke.

"I wonder what they'll think about being the godparents to our baby?" she asked, her back going rigid as though she were bracing for impact.

"What?" he asked disbelievingly. "What did you just say?"

She stood up a little taller and kissed his cheek. "You heard me, Daddy." She let go of his shaking body and walked around the side of the car to kiss Maisie goodbye. "We'll see you tomorrow night."

"Enjoy your book," Maisie grumbled.

"We will." Jamie laughed, scooping Trixie up in his arms and spinning her around joyfully.

"What's going on?" Travis asked as they made their way back off the beach.

"I have the best life," Jamie said, cradling his wife in his arms and staring into her eyes. "I have the best life possible. That's what's going on."

He put Trixie back on her feet and eyed her again to make sure she was serious. When she simply nodded, he knew. He knew he was about to be the man his mother would have hoped she could make him. The man Travis believed he could be. And the man Trixie knew he always was. Life was about to start for him, and he was finally ready for it.

Continue reading The Rough Waters Series with Book 3, The Rising Storm

THE RISING STORM - PROLOGUE

Noah stared out the window of the airplane rather than look down at his watch. Why bother? He was still only fourteen hours through his twenty-six-hour travel schedule. The hum of the plane engine and dim lights made the time crawl by, especially since he couldn't seem to sleep very long. It gave him ample time to think, to consider and then reconsider many things. Every thought was like a tiny paper cut, sharp at first with a lingering dull ache he couldn't seem to get rid of.

One thought that kept haunting him was how little was left after his wife Rayanne had died. The car accident that took her life took so much of him as well. He was physically different, about twenty pounds lighter, but the weight wasn't the only thing he'd lost. His analytical brain kept trying to make this into some kind of math equation. Noah plus Rayanne equaled one whole. When they married they'd become a new unit of measure. Maybe it was cliché but two really did become one.

At some point their balance shifted; their identity as a

couple was not half and half anymore. Rayanne became the face of their relationship. She was the person who kept in touch, made plans, gave thoughtful gifts, and organized events. When people thought about Noah and Rayanne, they thought of her first.

So when she died three quarters of him went with her. She took all the social aspects, the friends, the relationships.

"Another water?" the stewardess offered, and he jumped, nearly spilling the water he still had left in his cup.

"No, thank you," he said, clearing his throat. What he really wanted was a gin and tonic, but he hadn't had a drop of alcohol since that night he nearly ended it all. He still couldn't believe he was one of those people. Before his wife died, if someone were to ask him if he'd ever consider suicide, he'd have laughed. That was for sick people, sad people, not someone like him. He was far too logical to think ending his life was the right choice, no matter the circumstances. But that was the shocking realization he was still struggling to swallow. Sad could appear out of thin air. That bottomless hole could open up under anyone's feet at any moment. No one was immune. No one was safe.

So like any other trial in his life, Noah formed a rational plan. Whatever he'd done wrong, every shortcoming he'd had during his marriage to Rayanne, he'd fix it now. That's why he was on this plane. Everyone else was probably looking for a way to leave the Palanie Islands by now. The storm had hit two weeks ago. The devastation was immeasurable, or so he'd been told. It was the strongest recorded storm to ever make landfall. Help was needed. The perfect place to prove he could be a better person.

Postponing the trip to help Jamie and Trixie had thrown some of his plans up in the air, but he was going to make it work. Noah was rarely derailed for long. He'd put his mind to this, and he was going to see it through.

Originally he'd planned a volunteer trip to Brazil. He thought he'd do some sightseeing, work, and get some perspective. Clear his mind while doing some good. He was scheduled to head to a small town that needed vaccinations and some general care but not much more. It was an adventure and, overall, a safe endeavor.

His mind changed when the first pictures of the impending super storm flashed across the news. Forecasters were anticipating monumental destruction. Like a whisper in his ear, Noah heard his wife's voice. If she were alive and saw the news she'd have cried. She'd have lost sleep thinking about all the people who would have been affected. That's who she was. She worried for people she'd never met who lived in places she'd never been.

Historically Noah lacked the capacity for that kind of empathy. He always believed there was no point to it. You couldn't help people by simply crying over their pain. Noah was deliberate in his life. Could he act? Could he make a difference? If not, he made little room for it in his life.

In retrospect it made him sick to his stomach to think how many times he'd laughed her emotion off or told her she was crazy. How heartless he'd been to her kindness. So like any other problem he had, he worked toward a solution. He called the charity's organizer and told her he was changing plans. He didn't need a sightseeing trip to Brazil. He needed to listen to the whisper in his ear. Over and over it echoed: Help them.

. . .

Continue reading The Rough Waters Series with Book 3, The Rising Storm

ALSO BY DANIELLE STEWART

Missing Pieces Series:

Book 1: The Bend in Redwood Road

Book 2: The Pier at Jasmine Lake

Book 3: The Bridge in Sunset Park

Book 4: The Stairs to Chapel Creek

Book 5: The Cabin on Autumn Peak

Book 6: The Shore at East Bonnet Beach

Book 7: The Field on Oakwood Farm

Book 8: The Skyscrapers of Triton Street

Brave Moments Series:

Book 1: Anywhere the Weeds Grow

Book 2: Anytime the Birds Fall

Book 3: Any Place the Sun Rises

Piper Anderson Series:

Book 1: Chasing Justice

Book 2: Cutting Ties

Book 3: Changing Fate

Book 4: Finding Freedom

Book 5: Settling Scores

Book 6: Battling Destiny

Book 7: Unearthing Truth

Book 8: Defending Innocence

Book 9: Saving Love (includes excerpts from Betty's Journal)

Edenville Series – A Piper Anderson Spin Off:

Book 1: Flowers in the Snow

Book 2: Kiss in the Wind

Book 3: Stars in a Bottle

Book 4: Fire in the Heart

Piper Anderson Legacy Mystery Series:

Book 1: Three Seconds To Rush

Book 2: Just for a Heartbeat

Book 3: Not Just an Echo

Broken Mirror Series:

Book 1: The Way Down

Book 2: The Way Home

Book 3: The Way Back

The Clover Series:

Hearts of Clover - Novella & Book 2: (Half My Heart & Change My Heart)

Book 3: All My Heart

Over the Edge Series:

Book 1: Facing Home

Book 2: Crashing Down

Midnight Magic Series:

Amelia

Rough Waters Series:

Book 1: The Goodbye Storm

Book 2: The Runaway Storm

Book 3: The Rising Storm

Stand Alones:

Yours for the Taking

****

Multi-Author Series including books by Danielle Stewart

All are stand alone reads and can be enjoyed in any order.

Indigo Bay Series:

A multi-author sweet romance series

Sweet Rendezvous - Danielle Stewart

Short Holiday Stories in Indigo Bay:

A multi-author sweet romance series

Sweet Holiday Traditions - Danielle Stewart

BOOKS IN THE BARRINGTON BILLIONAIRE SYNCHRONIZED WORLD

By Danielle Stewart:

Fierce Love

Wild Eyes

Crazy Nights

Loyal Hearts

Untamed Devotion

Stormy Attraction

Foolish Temptations

Surprising Destiny

Lovely Dreams

Perfect Homecoming

Promising Reunion

Unending Bliss

Fearless Protector

You can now download all the Barrington Billionaire books by Danielle Stewart in a "Sweet" version. Enjoy the clean and wholesome version, same story without the spice. If you prefer the hotter version be sure to download the original.

The Sweet version still contains adult situations and relationships.

Fierce Love - Sweet Version

Wild Eyes - Sweet Version

Crazy Nights - Sweet Version

Loyal Hearts - Sweet Version

Untamed Devotion - Sweet Version

Stormy Attraction - Sweet Version

Foolish Temptations - Sweet Version - Coming Soon

FOREIGN EDITIONS

The following books are currently available in foreign translations

German Translation:

Fierce Love

Ungezügelte Leidenschaft

Wild Eyes

Glühend heiße Blicke

Crazy Nights

Nächte, wild und unvergessen

Loyal Hearts

Herzen, treu und ehrlich: Die Welt der Barrington-Milliardäre

Untamed Devotion

Ungezähmte Hingabe

***

French Translation:

Flowers in the Snow

Fleurs Des Neiges

NEWSLETTER SIGN-UP

If you'd like to stay up to date on the latest Danielle Stewart news visit www.authordaniellestewart.com and sign up for my newsletter.

AUTHOR CONTACT INFORMATION

Website: AuthorDanielleStewart.com
Email: AuthorDanielleStewart@Gmail.com
Facebook: facebook.com/AuthorDanielleStewart
Twitter: @DStewartAuthor
Bookbub: https://www.bookbub.com/authors/danielle-stewart
Amazon: https://www.amazon.com/Danielle-Stewart/e/B00CCOYB3O

Made in the USA
Columbia, SC
09 July 2024